Vic fixed his gaze on hers. "Wannna do something crazy?"

Aubrey was already shaking her head.

“Hear me out.” He grinned. “Spend the night with me. No talk about the past or the future. We’ll do what we’re best at doing, feel that sweet release we’re both aching for, and in the morning you can pretend it never happened. What d’ya say?”

“I say you’re crazy,” she breathed, a visual of him kissing her deeply flashing through her mind.

He leaned close and dipped his voice into seductive territory.

“Remember how good we were together? I’ll deliver, mark my words. I’ll make it so good, you’ll forget your own name.”

Desire slid honey-smooth through her veins. She knew from experience Vic’s suggestive tone wasn’t for show.

“And then we go back to normal like nothing happened?”

“Hand to God.” He raised a palm. “We’ll never speak of it again.”

* * *

An Ex to Remember by Jessica Lemmon is part of the Texas Cattleman’s Club: Ranchers and Rivals series.

Dear Reader,

Bad boy Vic Grandin hasn't been the shiniest example of a hero in the past, and that includes the years he dated his high school sweetheart, Aubrey Collins. Ten years have passed since their final breakup, but an unlikely and unexpected event has occurred—Aubrey has lost a chunk of her memory, forgetting that she and Vic were ever apart.

Her well-meaning parents and doctor manage to convince Vic to reprise his role as Aubrey's boyfriend while she heals, which he agrees to do—for her. He knows he doesn't deserve a second chance, but being close to Aubrey (even temporarily) is too much temptation for him to resist.

I love a second chance story, and Vic and Aubrey's unique tale is no exception. I adored writing the setting of a Texas ranch, a bad boy who finds his way back to what's right and the challenges that arise when Aubrey eventually regains her memories. I hope you enjoy reading the story of how these two navigate the choppy waters back to one another as much as I enjoyed penning it.

Happy reading!

Jessica Lemmon

www.jessicalemmon.com

JESSICA LEMMON

AN EX TO REMEMBER

Special thanks and acknowledgment are given to Jessica Lemmon for her contribution to the Texas Cattleman's Club: Ranchers and Rivals miniseries.

ISBN-13: 978-1-335-58139-6

An Ex to Remember

For questions and comments about the quality of this book, please contact us at CustomerService@Harlequin.com.

Harlequin Enterprises ULC
22 Adelaide St. West, 41st Floor
Toronto, Ontario M5H 4E3, Canada
www.Harlequin.com

Printed in U.S.A.

A former job-hopper, **Jessica Lemmon** resides in Ohio with her husband and rescue dog. She holds a degree in graphic design, which is currently gathering dust in an impressive frame. When she's not writing supersexy heroes, she can be found cooking, drawing, drinking coffee (okay, wine) and eating potato chips. She firmly believes God gifts us with talents for a purpose, and with His help, you can create the life you want.

Jessica is a social media junkie who loves to hear from readers. You can learn more at jessicalemmon.com.

Books by Jessica Lemmon

Harlequin Desire

Dynasties: Beaumont Bay

Second Chance Love Song
Good Twin Gone Country

The Dunn Brothers

Million-Dollar Mix-Up
Million-Dollar Consequences

Texas Cattleman's Club

An Ex to Remember

Visit her Author Profile page at Harlequin.com, or jessicalemmon.com, for more titles.

You can also find Jessica Lemmon on Facebook, along with other Harlequin Desire authors, at Facebook.com/harlequindesireauthors!

One

At the bar of the Silver Saddle, Vic Grandin tipped a fresh bottle of ice-cold beer to his lips and let out a sigh. Tonight at the family ranch he'd gotten into it with his oldest sister, Chelsea, over—what else—who was going to be in charge of the place once Dad retired.

Butting heads with Chelsea over him being the "chosen one" was nothing new. She and Vic were oil and water and had been since the day he'd been born. His four-years-older sister was a force to be reckoned with, and it just so happened he was the reckoning who'd come to set her straight.

Dad had chosen to put Vic in charge. It'd been decreed from the day Victor Jr. and Bethany Grandin learned they were having a baby boy. Their *only* boy, as it turned out. Vic had three other siblings—all sisters—but none of them had given him the hell Chelsea had.

He pinched the bridge of his nose, figuring he wasn't going to come to a solution tonight any more than he'd skip the TCC charity pool party tomorrow. He hadn't been in a partying mood lately, but he was resigned to going. Attending the Texas Cattleman's Club parties was tradition in Royal, Texas. In other words: *mandatory for all members*.

Maybe it wouldn't be so bad. He could try his luck tomorrow and talk a curvy, bikini-clad woman into warming his sheets for the night. He'd been no stranger to strangers in his bed for the last decade or so. Why change now?

But a quiet voice inside warned that a hookup would be less satisfying than it sounded. He'd been on a sort of sexual hiatus for just that reason. Lately the company of a good woman—even for a night—had made him feel empty. A tough sell for a man who'd been seeking the rest of himself for as long as he could remember.

Before he could remind himself to snap out of his shitty mood, a musical voice wafted along the shining bar top, over his left shoulder, and dripped like honey into his ear canal. Beer bottle hovering in midair, he paused, allowing the sound to coat his body in a familiar, aching warmth. He knew that voice. The soft, kind quality of it when she was being polite, or the tremor of hurt it held whenever she was angry.

Aubrey Collins had never truly been capable of

meanness. During their long-deceased relationship, meanness had been reserved for him.

He turned his head after bracing himself for seeing her, but the sight of her still sent him into a spiraling, sputtering tailspin. Her profile—the cute nose, full pouty lips and long, carelessly styled auburn hair—served as reminders of all he'd lost. Those features were virtually the same as the day she'd thrown his engagement ring at him and told him under no uncertain terms to go fuck himself.

"Evening, Ms. Collins," he drawled, unwilling to let her flee the premises without first acknowledging his presence. He guessed their interaction wouldn't end well, and he'd likely feel like shit on the drive home as he remembered the hand he'd had in turning his starry-eyed good girl into a jaded, bitter woman.

Since Vic was no stranger to bad ideas with worse consequences, he wouldn't let her leave without talking to him. She'd either ignored him or avoided him over the years, but there'd been no missing hearing her ask for her take-out order a moment ago. He figured he had a few minutes, tops, to converse with his ex.

She faced him, smooth, fiery red hair sliding over one delicate shoulder. A shoulder covered with the capped sleeve of a floral dress. She looked every ounce the girl next door, but he knew beneath that tasteful frock lay a seductress who'd let loose with him more times than he could count. Now she was closer in proximity to him than she'd been in years, her green eyes flashing a warning not unlike the shake of a rattlesnake's tail. He wasn't scared. She couldn't hurt him any more after rejecting him so thoroughly years ago.

"Mr. Grandin." A regal eyebrow arched over grass-green eyes. They weren't piercing or sharp, but gentle. It was a dichotomy he hadn't expected when they'd met as teenagers, much like her red hair didn't equal a hot temper. Though with him, she had managed to argue damn well. And hold a damn good grudge.

He spun the beer bottle in his hand and tried for small talk. "What brings you out tonight?"

"Takeout. I had a craving for dessert, and no one does cannoli better than Bo."

Cannoli. She loved the dessert, with its cinnamony shell and sweet ricotta filling. Bo went the extra mile and topped it with fresh whipped cream, house-made chocolate sauce and a cherry, which was likely why Aubrey had come here to buy the confection. Or it could be that it was nearing nine at night and the bakeries around town were closed.

"I hear you're announcing the chili cook-off winners tomorrow," he said, opting to stick to what little they had in common. Sadly, their attendance at the event was about all they had left.

She turned her body toward him, curves subtle but visible in the simple dress. Short cowboy boots were on her feet, which made him remember how they used to ride together on his horse whenever she visited the ranch. The wind would blow her hair, and his senses would be filled with the soft fragrance of wildflowers and Aubrey. She was standing two seats down from him, but the electricity that had always zapped between them hummed in the air all the same. He'd felt that way the first day he'd laid eyes on her. She'd been a high school freshman and he was a sophomore with no idea how fucking lucky he was about to be. His luck would eventually run out, and faster than he would have liked.

"Announcing the winner is an honor bestowed upon teacher of the year, you know." She feigned vanity as she flipped her hair. Hair that had tickled his cheek when he'd first kissed her, and later, his chest—and lower—when he'd talked her into doing a host of bad-girl things with him. She'd turned him into a shuddering, brainless mess back in the day. He'd bet she still could.

Damn memories. What he wouldn't give to lose every last one of them where she was concerned. The great ones only reminded him of worse ones. What was the point?

"I heard. Congratulations." He hated the bend of their bland conversation, but he was out of time. Her name had been called by a hostess, who came from the direction of the kitchen carrying Aubrey's to-go order.

"Thank you. It included an honorary TCC membership for the remainder of the year, so looks like we'll be seeing each other around."

He ignored the skipped beat of his heart. Would she show up with a date to future TCC engagements? He didn't know if he could tolerate seeing her with another man.

Her smile for the hostess was genial as she took the paper bag by the handles. She offered him the same smile and paired it with a generic "Good to see you." Like she was talking to a mailman or a clerk rather than the man she used to love with her entire being. He refused to let this opportunity pass without doing something. *Anything.*

"Why don't you let me buy you a drink? You can eat your cannoli here." He had no idea where that ill-fated suggestion had come from, but he doubled down, pulling out the high-backed stool next to his at the bar. "I promise I'll be nice."

Fingers looped around the paper bag's handles, she let out a disbelieving laugh. "*Nice* is not a description of Vic Grandin one hears very often."

"No, I s'pose not. Come on." He slapped the seat for emphasis. "One drink."

She was thinking about it. He could tell by the way she tipped her head and pursed those luscious lips. Lips he suddenly needed on his more than another sip of beer. If he could talk her into staying for a drink, maybe he could talk her into more. What'd be the harm in one kiss?

She glanced at the exit, as if calculating how long it'd take for her to sprint to her vehicle, before looking back at him. She shook her head, and that's when he knew he'd convinced her. She held up her index finger. *"One."*

His heart leaped like he'd scored the winning touchdown in the big game. He couldn't stop his grin as he ordered her a chardonnay from the bartender.

"Actually, I'll have a martini. On the rocks, extra dry. Two olives." She turned keen eyes on his as she pulled a plastic container from the bag. "Seems you don't know me as well as you think you do."

"Seems so." Vic blew a laugh from his lips and watched the bartender make a drink he'd never in his life seen Aubrey order. When she pried off the lid to her dessert, he leaned close, catching a whiff of her clean-cotton scent. "Are you gonna share that with me or what?"

"Or what," she replied, her smile painted on. At least that's what her smile felt like. Like she'd slapped on a faux joker's grin from cheek to cheek. She'd had a long week, and all she'd wanted tonight was to sit down with a bottle of wine and her favorite movie. First, she'd eaten dinner—a salmon Caesar salad she'd made herself—but by the time she'd reached for the wine, the idea of a cannoli from the Silver Saddle had introduced itself into her mind and refused to leave.

Now she was here, a martini she didn't want in front of her, and she was eating dessert with a man she didn't particularly like. She used to love him, but that'd been a long time ago.

She sipped the bitter drink and licked her lips, vowing to choke it down for the sake of her pride. Vic wasn't allowed to presume what she needed or wanted out of life. Not anymore. She was no longer the innocent sixteen-year-old who'd been enamored with him, or the eighteen-and-a-half-year-old who'd practically begged him to take her virginity. Hell, she wasn't even the twenty-year-old who'd bounced her engagement ring off his chest after a horrible argument.

She was thirty now, an adult. Teacher of the year. Honorary TCC member. Single, sure, but no longer ignorant of the ways of the world. And she had a PhD in Vic Grandin. She knew beneath that charm there was a man who relished having control. A man who believed he was God's gift to everyone.

But. She'd grown up and understood that punishing him with the cold-shoulder treatment wasn't helping her evolve as a person. She saw him around Royal often—how could she not when the Grandin family roots ran four generations deep into their ranch land? She'd see him at the TCC pool party tomorrow, and again next month at the Halloween masquerade, and, oh, don't forget the Christmas festivities. Perhaps she should have refused the offer of membership…

As unpalatable as the idea of forced conversations with him was, she was done keeping to herself. She had a life, too. Accepting the offer to announce the chili cook-off winners was only the beginning of her being out and about more. She and Vic might as well call a truce. She took another drink of her disgusting martini, narrowly avoiding a shudder.

"Since when do you drink martinis?" he asked, sounding unsure.

"A while now," she lied. "I see you haven't veered from the same red-labeled beer you were drinking when you were underage."

"Don't fix what's not broken." He sucked on the beer bottle, his throat moving as he swallowed. She took a good look at him up close. From dark wavy hair she knew was soft to the touch to espresso-brown eyes she'd sworn she'd glimpsed her future in. His solid build had filled out some, but his jeans and flannel shirt and the boots hooked on the rung of the chair hadn't changed a bit. She shouldn't admire him but couldn't help herself. This was Royal. She could throw a rock and hit a guy wearing a flannel and boots, but Vic looked better than any Texan had a right to. Especially given how well she knew him.

They drank and chatted about his parents and hers, his family's ranch and what it was like for her to teach high schoolers. Maybe it was the martini loosening her limbs, but she found herself relaxing into the conversation. Leaning on one elbow, she finally surrendered the dessert container to him.

"Really?" His smile was one of delight, sending a strange jolt of awareness through her. From her chest to her belly to parts too long neglected to acknowledge.

While she hadn't been much of a partygoer over the years, she had kept busy with work. Her passion for teaching followed her home like a stray puppy, one she welcomed and nurtured. That meant a lot of nights spent planning and grading, but her students were worth it. They, and her career, had become Aubrey's whole life. Which meant dating had taken a back seat. She'd made some effort to date over the last ten years she and Vic had been apart, but not as much as he had. *Nowhere* near as much as he had.

"Hurry before I change my mind." She offered him her spoon.

"I haven't eaten one of these in ages."

He polished off the remaining cannoli in two

bites, licking a dollop of whipped cream from the spoon. Watching his tongue swipe the sweet cream from his upper lip shook her good sense from her head like a cup full of dice. She remembered how he'd lain waste to her with that tantalizing mouth… when he hadn't been bossing her around with it.

He plucked the cherry from the container, still dripping with chocolate sauce, ate it, and then dangled the empty stem between them. Narrowing one eye, he asked, "Think I can still do it?"

"With the practice you've had over the last ten years?" She folded her arms and tried to appear not to care that he'd been with other women since her. She *shouldn't* care. "I bet you can do it with your eyes closed."

"I'll take that bet." He closed his eyes, dark lashes casting shadows on his cheeks, and popped the stem into his mouth. As he worked his jaw, she took advantage of the moment and soaked him in. His handsome face, the bad-boy scruff that had been absent when he'd dated her and the divot in his chin she'd always found unforgivably sexy.

He opened his eyes and caught her staring, his schoolboy grin as mischievous as the day he'd asked her out after class that first time. Then he produced the cherry stem between his teeth. He'd tied it in a knot with his tongue, which ushered in more memories of how good he'd been with that part of his anatomy when they'd been together.

He held the knotted stem between his index finger and thumb and fixed his gaze on hers. "Wanna do something crazy?"

Too late.

"Like what?" she heard herself ask. There was a rogue part of her chanting, "Do it, do it!" Entertaining that voice was as ill-advised as having a drink with Vic in the first place. *That's it. No more martinis.*

"Like relive our past. The good part. The best part."

She was already shaking her head.

"Hear me out, Aubrey with the auburn hair." He grinned. She couldn't help smiling at the nickname he'd sung loudly and obnoxiously whenever he'd passed her in the hallway on her way to Advanced English. His voice low and husky, he rumbled, "Spend the night with me. No talk about the past or the future. We'll do what we're best at doing, feel that sweet, sweet release we're both aching for, and in the morning you can pretend it never happened. What d'ya say?"

"I say you're crazy," she breathed while a visual of him kissing her deeply, his hand beneath her bra, danced merrily in her brain. The worst part was that she wasn't half as offended as she should be.

"Yeah, I am. But who cares?"

Why, oh, why was she considering his offer? She'd be insane to hop into bed with him again—certifiable. He somehow read her expression—or maybe her thoughts—and gave her the nudge that would seal her fate. After checking if anyone in the mostly empty bar was listening—they weren't—he leaned close and dipped his voice into seductive territory.

"Remember how good we were together, Aub? I'll

deliver, mark my words. I'll make it *so* good, you'll forget your own name."

She had to chuckle at his audacity, even as desire slid honey-smooth through her veins. It'd been a long time since anyone had delivered on half that promise. She knew from experience Vic's suggestive tone wasn't for show. Ten years hadn't dulled the white-hot memories from when they were naked together.

"And then we go back to normal like nothing happened?" She put her hand to her throat and toyed with her necklace, hardly able to believe her own ears.

"Hand to God." He raised a palm. "We'll never speak of it again."

Two

Two days later

Aubrey blinked her eyes open and instantly wanted to shut them again. Her head ached, but it wasn't a normal ache. It wasn't like when she slept on her neck wrong or spent too much time looking down at her laptop. It was a full skull ache, with battering rams and spikes that'd been driven in by sledgehammers. She reached up to touch her temple, and that's when she encountered the bandage. Not a huge white gauze wrapped Van Gogh style, but a decent-size patch covering some sort of injury.

Also, she was not in her bedroom at home, recovering from too many Vic-induced orgasms. She was…in a hospital room?

Her mother leaned over Aubrey's supine form, worry lines bisecting her fair strawberry-blond eyebrows. "How did you sleep?"

"Um." Aubrey looked around at the muted tan walls, the uninspired abstract floral paintings, and finally down at the scratchy white sheets and avocado-green throw covering her lower half. Even in a suite, with no need for a privacy curtain, there was no missing that she was in a hospital bed. Aubrey shut her eyes and tried to think back on what could have landed her in here, but her mind was a literal blank. "What happened?"

Her mother's gaze slid to the side, where Aubrey's father, Eddie, stood, his smile broadcasting as much worry as Mary's frown. He was a gentle man, and Aubrey had always been Daddy's girl, but the tenderness with which he looked at her was scaring her a little.

"You took a spill, gingerbread," he said, using her nickname from when she was a small girl. "Just a light knock on the head. But we couldn't be too careful."

"Oh." She didn't have any memory of the "spill" she'd taken. Patchy memories would be concerning, but she didn't even have those. "Where was I when it happened?"

"It doesn't matter, dear," her mother said, which was a weird response.

"Of course it matters." Aubrey pushed her hands into the mattress and sat straighter, earning a spike of pain down the back of her skull for her trouble. She held her head in her hands and breathed deeply, her eyes settling on the blanket and the matching avocado-green gown she was wearing. "I can't remember what happened. That's a problem."

"It's not as bad as you might think." A throaty female voice entered the room ahead of the woman who owned it. The doctor had a full, friendly face and sleek black hair, and she was at least an inch taller than Aubrey's father. She carried an iPad in one hand, which she glanced down at as she introduced herself. "I'm Dr. Mitchell. How are you feeling?"

"I— My head hurts. And I can't remember falling. Is anything broken?"

"No broken bones. The cut on your head was minor. You can probably lose that bandage in a few days." Dr. Mitchell hummed as she scrolled through her tablet. "I see you fell during the chili cook-off at a pool party of some kind."

"The TCC charity pool party," Aubrey said automatically, but she didn't recall being there, only that she'd had it on her schedule. "I was announcing the winners, right?"

"The stage collapsed while you were at the podium," the doctor answered calmly. "You were knocked unconscious, which can be very serious. Overall, your scans looked good, and there is no swelling in the brain. It's normal to have gaps in your memory in the meantime. They should return little by little."

"Gaps? How many gaps?" Aubrey's heart raced as she absorbed the news. She fell and knocked herself unconscious? Her memory *should* return? None of it sounded like good news to her. Her parents were wearing twin expressions of worry, and the doctor was talking to Aubrey like she was younger than the sixteen-year-old students she taught. A wave of relief covered her as she realized she remembered that, at least. She was a teacher, high school. Advanced Writing 101. "I was voted teacher of the year."

"Well, that is some accomplishment. Congratulations." The doctor offered a pretty smile that reached her eyes. Aubrey wanted to trust her, but she was having trouble not fleeing from the room in a panic. "It's important for you to rest. Take it easy."

"The school year just started," Aubrey huffed. "I have lesson plans. I have students counting on me to—"

"You have to rest, honey," her mother said. "Doctor's orders."

Aubrey turned to Dr. Mitchell and pleaded with her eyes.

"I can't allow you to return to school until I'm satisfied you've recovered. I suggest you stay with your parents for the foreseeable future. They told me they have plenty of space."

"I repainted the guest room," Mary Collins chirped.

"No, Mom. I…I'll stay in my apartment." Wherever that was, she thought as another dart of panic embedded itself in her chest.

"I'm sorry, Aubrey. You can't be alone right now," the doctor said.

"Well, then I'll stay with Vic." That made the most sense. She wasn't moving home like some prepubescent child. "Where is he, by the way?"

Her mother's jaw dropped while her father's mouth pulled into a tight line of disapproval.

"Vic's not welcome here," her father growled. She knew Vic wasn't her father's favorite person, but it was about time he got over it. They'd been dating for nearly fifteen years at this point.

"You have no right to keep him from me. He's my boyfriend. I love him. I need him, especially since I can't remember anything." She squeezed her eyes shut and pounded her balled fist on her leg. Her eyes sprang open, her heart thrashing as a memory descended. "We were eating cannoli together the night before the pool party."

"Vic?" her mother asked.

"Yes, Vic!" Aubrey laughed, thrilled to have uncovered a recent memory. "Then we..."

One look around the room reminded her she shouldn't share what happened after. The moment he'd taken her hand and led her from the Silver Saddle. They'd driven separately, for reasons she couldn't recall, so he'd followed her to her apartment. He'd kissed her the second she let them inside, his hands sliding around her waist. He'd tasted like vanilla whipped cream and heaven. She remembered the rest of the night in vivid Technicolor. The way he'd taken off her clothes slowly, kissing every revealed patch of skin. How he'd murmured compliments and encouragement into her ear while he made love to her in her bed. He'd stayed over but left early the next morning, kissing her goodbye and leaving a mug of coffee on the nightstand as she lay blissfully sated and hugging her pillow.

"We…hung out," she finished lamely. "Anyway, I need to see him."

"I think that would be a splendid idea." The doctor's eyes twinkled before she turned to Aubrey's parents. "Can you give Vic a call? Tell him to swing by, that Aubrey is well enough to see him and is asking for him."

"He's probably worried sick." Aubrey figured that must be true. After the night they'd shared, how could he not be here? "I don't understand why he's not by my side. That's not like him."

She shook her head, trying to will forth more memories, but there was a significant gap where Vic was concerned. While she recalled the sensual night they spent together with pulse-racing clarity, the last memory of him before that one was when they'd been in high school together. Although, that sort of made sense. They'd fallen in love during those tender early years, so those memories were embedded in her brain deeper than most. But she couldn't shake the idea that there should be more mundane memories. Of dinners out and coffees at his ranch. Of I-love-you phone calls or text messages while she was at school.

"I'm scared," she said to her shaking hands. "I can't seem to remember much at all. What if my memory never comes back? What kind of life can I lead living in the dark?"

"Try not to worry." The doctor placed a hand over both of Aubrey's. "Remember what I said. Don't try too hard and they will come. I've worked with many patients who have suffered head trauma. This isn't as uncommon as you might think."

"It's not?"

"Nope. Your brilliant brain knows what it's doing. In the meantime, we're going to call Vic. Get him right over here."

Aubrey nodded. Panic wasn't going to help her heal any sooner, but she couldn't stop the anxiety from descending. Her parents exchanged concerned glances, and she shook her head, not understanding why they were trying to keep Vic away from her.

"He probably had an emergency at the ranch. He's got a lot on his plate." She had no specific recollection as evidence that was true, but it felt true. She was going to have to trust the rest of her senses in the absence of memories.

"I'll prescribe meds for the headache," the doctor told her as she tapped her iPad. Then she turned to Aubrey's parents. "If you have a moment, I can explain Aubrey's medicine and a few guidelines she needs to follow."

"Sure," Mary answered, Eddie by her side.

"Mind if I borrow your parents and send in a nurse to treat your headache, Aubrey?"

"That's fine. As long as you come right back with Vic." She aimed that command at her father, who gave her a solemn nod.

"All right, gingerbread."

Vic had given up pacing in the waiting room an hour ago. Now he sat on the uncomfortable chair and bobbed one knee up and down while he checked his email on his phone. Trying to work remotely was a waste of time, but he needed to occupy his mind while he waited to see Aubrey. Without the distraction of social media or work, all he'd done was worry himself sick. He wasn't leaving this hospital until he saw she was okay with his own two eyes.

At the chili cook-off, she had taken the stage, looking more gorgeous than the night before, when he'd slipped into bed with her at her apartment. He'd promised they'd never speak of it again, but the moment her bright green eyes landed on his, he'd decided to hell with his promise. He'd planned on waiting until she announced the winners and scooping her into his arms. He didn't give a shit who saw—his best friend, Jayden, his sisters or Aubrey's parents. But his plans hadn't worked out.

Just as she'd begun her speech, the stage crashed down on one side, sending Aubrey flying off it. Vic had pushed his way through the crowd that had been closing in collectively to help. By the time he reached Aubrey, her mother was on the phone with 911 and Eddie Collins was telling him to "stay the hell away from my daughter."

Vic had been on the brink of telling her father that his daughter had been sleeping in his arms not twenty-four hours ago, but Jayden had rushed in and restrained him. Good thing, too, or who knew what sort of scene Vic would have made.

Instead, he'd fallen back, waiting as Aubrey was checked by paramedics and then following the ambulance to the hospital. Jayden had insisted on going with him, but Vic refused. The accident had shifted the vibe of the evening from best friends each looking for a woman to share the night with to one of concern and worry.

What Vic hadn't told his best bud was that he *hadn't* been looking for a woman to share the night with. Not after spending the previous night with Aubrey. Feeling her beneath him for the first time in ten years had been nothing short of a miracle, and miracles didn't occur often in his life. Holding her in his arms, her breaths tickling his neck as she slept soundly, he'd decided his life had been shitty for far too long. As grateful as he was for his wealth, his community status and his family, a piece was missing. Could Aubrey be that piece?

When Vic had rushed to the hospital behind the ambulance, he'd been told to sit in the waiting room. He'd pushed his luck, approaching anyone wearing scrubs, telling everyone who would listen that he needed to see his fiancée. A white lie, but one he'd hoped would gain him access faster.

Finally a thin, angular blonde nurse had come out to assure him that Aubrey was fine, but her doctor was limiting her visitors. Vic hit the roof. He'd used plenty of swear words to communicate how dissatisfied he was with that answer. That's when Eddie had emerged from a long hallway and threatened to call the cops.

Vic had laughed as he'd explained to Eddie that the cops in Royal wouldn't touch him. Everyone knew Victor Jr. would have their asses if they laid a hand on his only son. If pressed, Vic could make one phone call and have complete access to Aubrey's room—hell, this entire hospital. Then Aubrey's mother, Mary, had stationed herself between them. In a calm, motherly tone, she'd explained that the doctor's advice was designed to protect Aubrey. Mary had placed a hand on his arm and had said, "If you care about her, you'll cooperate."

It was a low blow, but she'd forced his hand. Vic promised to behave, adding the caveat that he wouldn't leave the waiting room until he was allowed to see her.

Now, after having spent several restless hours alternating between sitting on an uncomfortable chair or wearing the carpet to threads with his frantic pacing, Vic wasn't sure if he could keep the first half of his promise. He couldn't sit here another second without an update.

When he was halfway to the nurses' station, the nurse readied her frown for him as Mary and Eddie materialized from the corridor. He rerouted and raced to them, trying to read their expressions and failing. Was it worry he saw on Mary's face, or fatigue? Was Eddie angry simply because he'd been angry at Vic for the last decade, or had something awful—*more awful*—happened to Aubrey?

"What's wrong? What's going on?" Acid hit the back of Vic's throat thanks to too many cups of stale hospital coffee.

"She's awake, and she's asking for you." Eddie didn't sound happy about the fact. The man had his reasons, but Vic wasn't letting that stop him.

"Good. Let's go."

"Before you go in, we have to talk," came the

calm cadence of the doc who appeared at Mary's side. She extended an arm. "I'm Dr. Mitchell."

He shook the older woman's hand and listened while she explained Aubrey's state. Memory loss, at least partial, was described in medical terminology that didn't make Vic feel any better.

"Like brain damage?" he clarified, wondering if he might puke on the nice doctor's shoes.

"Her scans don't show any permanent damage, but the brain is tricky. Memories return in a trickle or a flood, but it's best that Aubrey remembers at her own pace, without anyone overwhelming her with facts in an effort to jog her memory."

"But she's asking for me, so she must remember me." Vic glanced at Mary.

"She remembers you." Mary smiled. Aubrey's mother had always liked him more than Eddie had. "And us. And that she's a high school teacher. She doesn't remember the fall…and a few other things."

Like the night we slept together?

"Aubrey believes you are a couple," the doctor interjected. "Her parents tell me you haven't been together for a long while."

"Ten years," Eddie put in.

"That's…not entirely true," Vic mumbled. Eddie's face hardened.

"Well, it's important to do what's best for Aubrey." Dr. Mitchell made deliberate eye contact with Aubrey's parents and then with Vic. "It's my recommendation to let her come to her memories on her own, but in the meantime, you should go along with what she believes is true."

"Seriously?" Vic asked, trying to wrap his head around this new twist.

"As long as it's not harming her in any way." Dr. Mitchell smiled.

"You don't know him." Aubrey's father glared at Vic.

"Eddie!" Mary admonished her husband. Then to Vic explained, "Too many facts too fast could overwhelm her and cause a setback, or worse."

"What could be worse?" Vic asked, his voice cracking.

"Right now she remembers quite a bit," the doctor continued. "Her vocation, the people around her. She mentioned her lesson plans and how she needs to return to work. There's no way I can clear her yet, but if she makes substantial progress, soon. Rest and consistency are the two most important aspects of her healing. She can take part in other activities, though I'd like her to avoid spending too much time with electronics—no binge-watching television shows or scrolling through social media on her cell phone."

"She's staying with us until she's better," Mary told Vic. He nearly laughed. Aubrey loved her parents, but when she left for college, she'd shared with him how she was glad to finally have her independence.

"I understand you have a ranch, Vic," said Dr. Mitchell.

"Yes."

"No horseback riding until I say."

He opened his mouth to agree when Eddie growled, "She's not going to be spending time with him."

"She can do whatever she damn well pleases," Vic growled back.

"Listen." The doctor held up both hands. "I'll reiterate, this is not about you or what you want for Aubrey. This is about what's best for *her*. So while your manly show of territorialism is very impressive, you are going to have to take a step back and allow Aubrey to be in the lead. She's a capable, intelligent woman who has suffered a hiccup in her memory. If you behave yourselves, she'll have a better chance of fully recovering that memory. Which is what we all want, right?"

"Right." Eddie answered first and spoke to Vic next. "And when her memory returns, she'll recall the hell you put her through. Then she won't want anything to do with you. The doc's right. My daughter's smart. She knows what's best for her. She knew ten years ago, too, and it wasn't you."

Vic stepped into Aubrey's hospital room alone, thank God. He hadn't been sure what to expect, though he wasn't surprised by her washed-out skin and limp hair, red-rimmed eyes and hospital gown. What did surprise him was her reaction when she saw him. She immediately started to cry.

He rushed to her side, and she grabbed his hand, kissing and nuzzling his knuckles. She told him how scared she was and asked why he hadn't been here earlier. She mentioned she'd been afraid he'd forgotten about her.

"I was here. I was in the waiting room. They wouldn't let me in." He sat on the edge of her bed.

Leaning over her came naturally, as did the temptation to kiss her. He resisted. Her gaze was locked on his, her eyes open and vulnerable. That was a recent development. Even after they'd slept together two nights ago, she hadn't looked at him with this sort of raw trust in her eyes. She'd had her guard way up. Hell, they both had. The release and afterglow of sex had been worth any discomfort that followed, but they had each been careful not to reveal too many of their secrets that night.

This tenderer version of Aubrey had been missing for a decade. She seemed genuinely relieved to see him, her hand stroking his forearm the way she used to whenever she was anxious.

"I can't believe my dad kept you from seeing me. He's ridiculous."

Rather than agree, which Vic did, he said, "I'm here now."

"Good." She sniffled and smiled. "Bust me out of here, will you?"

"As soon as I can," he promised. She wouldn't do well confined to this room, that was for sure. "Your doctor's a smart lady. She knows what's best for you."

"She said it'll take a while to regain my memory." Aubrey shook her head and looked out the window. "Amnesia, Vic. Like a damn Lifetime movie."

He had to chuckle. She was sure acting like herself—her wry sense of humor in place, her vulnerability, her pinpoint honesty. She was going to be fine. He'd make sure of it. If he had to scour the entire state of Texas—or the world—for a medical team who could help her recover, he would.

Though her father's promise that she would hate Vic once she regained her memory gave him pause. Vic wasn't so stupid to think she'd live and let live once she remembered the way they'd broken up back in the day. It was probably best to trust Dr. Mitchell, and in the meantime, Vic would provide what Aubrey wanted whenever she wanted it. Right now, miraculously, she wanted him.

He'd take that second chance, short-lived though it might be. He'd take that all the way to the bank.

Three

"I wish you'd let me help," Aubrey complained from her parents' wide front porch. She held the front screen door open for her father, who wrestled the remainder of her luggage into the house.

Her mother bustled in after him, arms loaded up with a vase of fresh, colorful flowers, a teddy bear with a ribbon around its neck, and several novels. All gifts from Vic, as he'd visited her routinely while she'd been forced to stay in the hospital for observation. The longest week of her life. Especially without the distraction of television or her cell phone. She hadn't been able to read much, either, thanks to her head hurting if she concentrated for longer than fifteen minutes.

"You're not allowed to help." Her mother winked

as she issued the warning for the second time. "Stop being so stubborn."

"I'm not." Aubrey followed them inside with a shake of her head. She hadn't magically regained her memory during that week of abject boredom, but the nurses and her doctor assured her that patience was key.

She trailed behind her parents as they dropped off her things in her old bedroom, now a guest room. The days of posters taped to the wall and rows of journals and stationery on the desk were long gone. Her mother had chosen a sophisticated color palette for the room. Muted blue-gray tone for the duvet as well as one accent wall. The other walls were painted eggshell white, including an upcycled dresser and the nightstands on either side of the double bed.

"It's like a hotel." Aubrey poked her head into the recently painted bathroom. "You said you were remodeling, but I had no idea it would look this different. Unless I'm forgetting?"

"No, no." Her mother waved her off. "You haven't seen it yet. I just did it!"

"Well, I like it." It would have to do, since Aubrey wasn't able to return to her apartment yet. Her apartment, which was decorated in the colors… She paused, her hand frozen on the bathroom light switch as she tried to picture her apartment.

Nothing.

"You all right, dear?" Mary asked.

"Yes. Totally fine." But Aubrey wasn't fine at all. She'd called up a blank rather than being able to picture her own bedroom. The way she'd called up blanks in many areas of her life. Some moments were crystal clear and bright. Others were lost in a black, cavernous void.

"I'll start dinner. Come on, Eddie. I need you to fire up the flattop grill for the steaks."

Her parents wandered down the hallway chatting as Aubrey knelt to unzip one of the suitcases her mother had packed for her. As she unearthed her clothes, she instantly felt better. The patterns and styles were familiar, and she recognized a college sweatshirt as one of her favorite go-to garments. She found lots of sleeveless shirts, her preference, as they showed off arms she worked out regularly at her apartment's fitness center. Her mother had also packed several dresses, floral patterned and solids alike. Aubrey usually paired her floral dresses with cowboy boots—check—or with her favorite brown sandals. She lifted a jacket and found them, the same pair she'd envisioned, at the bottom of the suitcase. Hugging the shoes to her chest, she shut her eyes and tried to picture walking into her closet.

Again, nothing.

She blew out a sigh and reminded herself not to rush. Dr. Mitchell had discouraged her from trying too hard, which had caused several headaches already. Aubrey had hoped she'd be able to picture something as mundane as a closet, though. Maybe if she instead thought of being in her bedroom… Eyes still closed, she pictured Vic setting a mug of coffee on the nightstand right before he kissed her goodbye. The memory bloomed to life on the backs of her eyelids.

"I'm taking off. I made you coffee." His voice was

low and rocky. His sexy morning voice. It seemed like eons since she'd heard it.

"Okay." She opened her eyes to take one last look at him. He was wearing last night's jeans and flannel. He needed to shave, but then again, no, he didn't. She preferred a bit of growth on that firm jaw of his. As long as he didn't grow it out too long to completely hide the divot in his chin, she wouldn't complain. Not to mention how talented he was with the mouth surrounded by that scruff. She could still feel it grazing the insides of her thighs...

"Mmm." She opened her eyes and smiled as the puzzle pieces slid together. Vic had walked out of her bedroom while she'd hugged her pillow and watched his very fine ass retreat down the hallway. She could picture the decor of her bedroom clearly now: crisp, clean navy blue and white, with framed black-and-white photographs hanging on the wall. One of a mountaintop, one of a steer peeking through a wire fence.

She *remembered.*

She'd sat up in bed and sipped her coffee, several naughty and delicious details of that night dancing in her head. Sex with Vic had been exquisite. From the moment he'd peeled off his shirt and revealed a tanned, thick chest. So familiar and yet so different from when they'd first been together. To the moment he'd slipped her out of her clothes and laid his lips on her collarbone. Her skin had sizzled the moment his mouth touched her bare flesh, and when he'd pulled one of her nipples onto his tongue, she'd nearly burst into flames.

She remembered their night together, all right.

None before it, which was odd, unless she counted her early college years. There seemed to be an awfully wide gap in her recollection…

"Progress is progress," she said aloud, pushing out the threat of panic. Dr. Mitchell had told Aubrey to expect her memory to come back gradually. She'd take the small progress she'd made today as a win. She wasn't going to beat herself up for not remembering everything all at once.

She stored her clothes in the dresser and hung her dresses in the closet. At least she'd remembered her evening with Vic—an entirely lovely memory.

Downstairs, she found her mother chopping vegetables for a salad. Aubrey nudged her out of the way and began slicing cucumbers into neat rounds, unreasonably satisfied when the slices were even. She hadn't lost her ability to cut veggies, or walk, or chew. She had so much to be grateful for.

"What time's dinner?" she asked her mom.

"Forty minutes or so. I have mac and cheese in the oven. That'll take the longest."

"I love your mac and cheese. I'll let Vic know."

Knife poised over a tomato, Mary regarded her daughter with raised eyebrows. "I'm not sure that's a good idea."

"Dad is going to have to learn to live with disappointment. Me being here is an adjustment for all of us, but I'm not changing my day-to-day lifestyle just because I'm under your roof. I'm thirty years old, and if I didn't have to be here, I wouldn't."

"Aubrey—"

"You can't keep me from seeing Vic because I'm

living here. This is a wild—and extenuating—circumstance."

It was ridiculous enough not to be allowed to go back to her apartment. Aubrey had argued about that, too, but had come to understand the doctor's reasoning. Dr. Mitchell had warned Aubrey that she could have a dizzy spell and fall in the shower or wake disoriented, having no idea what'd happened to her or where she was. The doctor had added that a familiar environment could overwhelm Aubrey with too much input, worsening her headaches or causing the memories she did have to retreat.

Losing more of her memory was unacceptable, so Aubrey agreed to bind and gag her independent nature for the sake of her healing. Anyway, her mom and dad were both retired teachers who were home most of the time, save for a few speaking engagements here or there. Staying with them would give Aubrey time with them, as well as someone looking over her who wasn't a nurse. It was the best solution. Well, not the *best.*

Aubrey had considered asking Vic if he had room at his place, but instinct warned her against mentioning it to him. They didn't live together, and there must be a reason. Plus, he was busy with the ranch most days. She refused to rattle around in his house—whatever that looked like—waiting for him to come home from work.

She was certain he'd invite her over soon enough, and then she could close another gap in her memory. They could make new memories of being in bed together while they were at it. A grin pulled at her lips.

"Just like when you lived here." Her mother clucked

her tongue. "You were over the moon for that boy then, and your father couldn't tell you otherwise."

"Why are they so angry with each other?" Aubrey frowned, unable to recall a plausible reason. "I know Dad's protective, but I'm not an innocent virgin any longer. Vic took that from me a long time ago."

"Aubrey!"

She laughed at her mother's cartoon expression of shock, bugged-out eyes and everything. "Come on, Mom. Don't act like you don't know Vic and I have—"

Aubrey's cell phone rang, saving her poor mother from further trauma. She reached into her shorts pocket and pulled out her phone, excited to see Vic's name on the screen.

"Hi, babe" came out of her mouth feeling both familiar and foreign at the same time. What an odd sensation.

"Hey, uh, Aub," he responded with the slightest hesitation. "Do you need anything, or do your parents have you settled?"

"I'm settled." She walked out the front door and stood on the porch, soaking in the eighty-five-degree weather. September in Texas was still summer, and felt like it. She loved the heat. The sun warmed her skin and reminded her she was alive, the day holding a million possibilities. "Would you like to come for dinner? Mom's making mac and cheese."

"I love your mom's mac and cheese," he answered, his voice low and sexy.

"After dinner you can take me out."

"Take you out?"

"Yes. *Out.* I've been wearing a hospital gown for a week, and I can't spend another minute with my doting parents. I am willing to be polite through dinner, but then you have to steal me away."

His rich laughter sent shivers to the surface of her skin in spite of the hot evening. "You sure you want me to do that?"

"Who else would I want to rescue me?" She paced around the outside of the house, admiring the thick bushes and colorful flowers surrounding her parents' pristine covered porch. Through a window she saw her mother bustling in the kitchen. "You could bring me to your place tonight. For some alone time."

There was a lengthy pause before he said, "I'm not sure you want to come to the ranch just yet."

She frowned. He still lived at the ranch? Granted, his family's home was massive. She remembered the stats—it was hard to forget a number like *sixteen thousand square feet.* The Grandin family home could easily house the entire family and more. With private entrances dotted throughout, she'd rarely stepped through the front door.

"Fine. I'll have to settle for you coming for dinner. We can drink iced tea on the porch, or you can take me out for ice cream after. I miss you."

He cleared his throat. "You do?"

"Yeah." Why wouldn't she?

"Ah, let me finish up and I'll be over. Can I bring anything?"

"Just your sexy self, in a perfectly tight pair of blue jeans. How'd that be?"

She heard the grin in his voice when he said, "Sounds good to me, sugar."

Vic ended the call with Aubrey and stared at the cell phone in his hand in wonder. He hadn't fully wrapped his head around what had transpired during the last week. Namely, that his ex missed him and wanted to spend the night with him.

"What was that about?" His sister Morgan echoed his thoughts as she stepped into his office. Two years younger than him, she was the sister who was almost always on his side. Likely because she didn't give a hoot or a holler—her words—about inheriting the ranch. She owned a fashion boutique called, aptly, The Rancher's Daughter. She knew what she wanted out of life, and it had nothing to do with raising cattle.

"Aubrey invited me to dinner at her parents' house."

"First you two hook up before the cook-off and now you're reconciling?"

Vic hadn't exactly shared that he and Aubrey had hooked up, but Morgan had questioned why he'd been at the hospital guarding Aubrey like a sentinel. He'd answered that they'd had dessert together before the cook-off, and then Morgan had rightly concluded, "Oh my God, you're sleeping together!"

He stood from his chair and grabbed his Stetson from the hook on the wall. He didn't always wear it, but today felt like a good day to start. He could hide his lying eyes beneath the brim. "She doesn't remember we're not a couple, Morgan. She's suffered a serious accident and is asking for my support. What the hell am I supposed to do?"

Morgan twisted her lips to one side. "It feels wrong."

It did. And yet completely right. There'd been a time when he'd have done almost anything for Aubrey. Showing up for her in her time of need felt as natural as breathing to him. "Don't worry. I won't take advantage of her."

Or take her to his bedroom in the private wing of the house, strip her naked and make love to her again. That sounded way too good to his own ears, especially since the memory of doing just that burned hot. But he refused to sleep with her when she had no idea they weren't a couple. The night after the Silver Saddle last week had been different—she'd known what she was getting into. And, damn, had they gotten into it.

Morgan's eyebrows bent as she twirled a lock of long red hair around a manicured fingertip. Unlike Aubrey's auburn locks, his sister's hair was pale red, her skin fairer. "I don't like lying to her."

"We're not lying to her," he said for his sister's benefit. "We're giving her room to remember on her own. Doctor's orders." He placed the hat on his head and sidled past her. "And for the record, I don't like it, either."

He left his office, shutting the door behind him and Morgan, and met his oldest sister, Chelsea, in the hallway, her folded arms and firm line for a mouth what he'd grown accustomed to.

"Say it quick," he warned. "I'm late for dinner with Aubrey's family."

"You're using her."

"I'm not," he said through clenched teeth.

"She hasn't given you the time of day for ten years, and you're waltzing into her life like you never left it."

"It hasn't been ten years. They were together recently," Morgan said in his defense.

"I have this, Morgan," he told his well-meaning but meddling sister. To Chelsea, he said, "Aubrey feels safe when she's with me. I'm doing what her parents and her doctor asked me to do."

"Safe? With you?" Chelsea laughed. "After you tried clipping her wings and making her the pretty little housewife of your dreams? If I recall, she dumped you for it."

"Well, Chels, I don't particularly care for your opinion on the matter."

"I didn't want your opinion on Nolan, either, baby brother."

He gritted his teeth. He'd done his fair share of poking his nose where it didn't belong in Chelsea's budding relationship with Nolan Thurston, but that was different. He'd been looking out for the family ranch, his legacy. "I have a second chance with her, and I'm taking it."

"You won't win her back." Chelsea raised an eyebrow.

"I'm not trying to win her back." He'd settle for her no longer hating him. More than that would be a stone-cold miracle, but her not hating him would be a solid start. Since he'd taken her to bed last week, he'd realized not having Aubrey in his life had reduced him to a primitive version of himself. He'd been growling at his family, lashing out in his own defense and metaphorically pissing on what he'd perceived as his territory.

He wasn't so arrogant as to think Aubrey would take him back, but if they could be cordial, and she could allow him to be in her life at some capacity, well, he thought he might be able to evolve into a halfway decent human being.

"I think it's sweet," Morgan said.

"Sweet!" Chelsea emitted another humorless laugh. "Vic, you are the most arrogant, self-centered man I've ever met, outside of Daddy. You are in this for *you* and no other reason."

His temper warmed his cheeks and caused his fists to curl into tight balls. He reminded himself that Chelsea had never understood him. She had long accused him of resting on his laurels while she did the heavy lifting at the ranch. For years she'd seen only what she wanted to see: that she was losing the ranch to her selfish brother. The truth was he did more than she'd bothered to give him credit for, but he also wasn't blameless. That was too big a discussion for the small amount of time allotted them in this moment.

"I gave up on trying to win your favor a long time ago, Chels." He wearily pushed past her and walked toward the exit. To Morgan, he said, "Don't wait up."

Four

Vic drove to Aubrey's parents' house, a doorstep he'd sworn never to darken again. He knew Chelsea was upset for reasons other than him lying to Aubrey, but he couldn't help feeling a tug of guilt at her accusation.

Chels never had approved of his confidence and didn't hesitate to remind him of his "cocky" nature. He'd be the first to admit his bullheadedness was a character flaw, but he'd come by it honestly. He'd inherited the art of stubbornness from his namesakes, his grandfather and his father. The third Victor in line, Vic had been entrusted to run one of the largest ranches in Royal, Texas, a job description that called for leadership.

Decisiveness and boldness were two qualities required for the ranch to stay profitable for generations to come. What Chelsea perceived as arrogance was Vic doing what their father had charged him to do. Taking over meant *taking over*, and that's exactly what Vic intended to do. If his sisters had been paying attention, they would've noticed that shit ran uphill, not down, when things went wrong. Being in charge was an enormous responsibility.

Not that it mattered at the moment. The family ranch wasn't stable. The question of whether or not there was oil beneath both the Grandin land and neighboring Lattimore property remained unanswered. Ever since a claim on the estate had been made by Heath Thurston, the land Vic called home had been threatened. If Heath seized the land, there'd be no family ranch for Vic, Chelsea and Layla to work.

A terrifying prospect.

He parked in the Collinses' driveway and shut off the truck. Leaning back in his seat, he considered how most people would not agree to play house with their ex. Vic wasn't like most people. The night they'd shared recently had been memorable enough that he'd show up wherever Aubrey asked him to. He wasn't a weak man, but when it came to his high school love, he didn't possess the strength to tell her no. Not when, in her fragile state, she looked at him like he'd hung the moon.

Nothing was better than when she smiled at him, as wide-eyed as when he'd first turned her head. Her admiration when they'd been teenagers had been infinitely better than the acrimony that'd followed years later.

During the long months following their split, he'd given up on winning her back. Eventually he'd reentered the dating world, but it hadn't taken long to realize that he wasn't going to find Aubrey's equal anywhere in this town—or the state. Hell, probably the whole damn solar system. So, fuck scruples. He was taking this opportunity to be in her circle for as long as she'd allow. He knew he still didn't deserve her, but it'd be nice to feel good for a while. It beat stressing out over the ranch while simultaneously handling the pressure of being the Grandin golden child.

At Eddie and Mary Collins's front door, Vic raised a fist to knock. He hid the bouquet of daisies behind his back, pleased when Aubrey opened the door instead of either of her parents. Her eyes were wide and excited before she saw the flowers, and then when she did, she melted like he'd brought her a dozen gold bars instead.

"They're for your mom. I hope you're not disappointed," he told her.

"I live here, too, so we'll both enjoy them." She grinned. It'd been her vibrant, sunshiny smile that had first hooked his heart. He hadn't seen it aimed at him for far too many years.

She clutched his wrist and dragged him into the house he hadn't seen since Aubrey left for college. No, he took that back. He'd come here once after they'd broken up. Vic had literally told Eddie he'd come to "talk some sense into her" for dumping him on his ass. Eddie hadn't let him inside, and Vic figured that'd been for the best. Any other attempts to reach her had been ignored or thwarted by her parents, and the rest was ancient history.

History Aubrey had *forgotten.*

"Mom, Vic's here. He brought you flowers." Aubrey released his arm and bustled around the kitchen filling a vase with water and unwrapping the daisies to arrange them on the dining room table. The same dining room table where he'd shared countless dinners with the Collinses when things had been good. The same sunken living room where they'd played Pictionary on a few innocent nights. The same plaid sofa where Vic and Aubrey had spent a not-so-innocent night while her parents had been away on vacation.

"Thank you, Vic. That's very thoughtful." Mary's mouth was a neutral line. She'd never been as angry at him as Eddie, but who had been? Even Aubrey hadn't matched her father's ire after she'd given the engagement ring back.

"Do you want a beer, babe?" It took Vic a second to realize Aubrey was addressing him.

"Sure."

She cracked the top off a red label and handed him the bottle. Then she pushed an empty platter into his other hand and shoved him toward the back deck. "Take this to Dad, will you? He'll need it for the steaks. Dinner's almost ready."

He couldn't say no to her sweet, sweet smile, despite her sending him into the lion's den.

Outside, Vic offered the platter. Eddie narrowed

his eyes but accepted it. Aubrey's father drank from his own beer bottle as he and Vic regarded the smoking grill in silence.

"Thanks for having me," Vic tried.

Eddie, his eyes on the steaks sizzling away on the flattop grill, squared his jaw. "We both know she deserves better than you."

That hadn't taken long.

"But you're who she needs right now. You, for some reason—" he waved the spatula in Vic's general direction "—bring her *joy*."

Vic, on the cusp of defending himself for doing exactly what Eddie—at the suggestion of the doctor—had asked Vic to do, was unexpectedly mollified by those words. Aubrey had forgotten their troubles and their shared pasts. Vic had been charged with standing in as her boyfriend to help her avoid further trauma. But joy? Joy was a tall order. When was the last time he'd brought a woman *joy*? The idea of it was a treasure he hadn't expected to find.

"I'd never lie to her if I could help it." Eddie flipped the steaks over to finish cooking. "Just so happens I can't help it. I love her more than anything on this earth."

"I understand, sir." And he did. At one point Vic had loved Aubrey more than anything on this earth, too. Before he'd screwed up and made her hate him. He was ashamed to admit that a fair amount of the bitterness between them had fueled some of his bad behavior in the past. That wasn't her fault, but at the time he'd laid some of the blame on her. And since he had yet to forgive himself for his repugnant behavior, the least he could do was be here to support her. Maybe he could make up for at least part of the pain he'd inadvertently caused her over the years.

"If for one moment I believe your presence is making her life harder—" Eddie began.

"Got it," Vic interrupted, cutting off whatever idle threat Eddie might make. Back when Vic and Aubrey were kids, Eddie's words had held less weight. Vic had believed he was above reproach with everyone. Now that he was older, and hopefully wiser, he understood her father's concerns.

What Eddie didn't know was that Vic intended to do whatever was best for Aubrey, and damn the consequences. If that meant going against Eddie's wishes, so be it.

"Have they killed each other yet?" Mary set the piping-hot casserole dish on a hot pad on the dining room table.

"Not yet." Aubrey backed away from the window before one or both men spotted her. So far she'd witnessed puffed chests and the swigging of beers. They weren't making eye contact. Dad was staring down at the smoking steaks like if he didn't watch the grill they might up and run for the Texas hills. Meanwhile, Vic was studying the sunset like it was his last before he went to live in an underground bunker.

"Dad sure can hold a grudge," she murmured as she joined her mother in the dining room.

"Your father has his reasons." Mary gave her daughter a pointed look as she fished silverware from the china hutch drawer.

Aubrey guessed her father's reasons were ones she should know, but there was a big empty space whenever she tried to remember why he didn't approve of Vic. Aubrey was his little girl, and he was as protective as usual, but her father's glower seemed to go beyond that reason.

"Steaks." Vic swaggered by and delivered the platter to the table. Aubrey's mouth watered, but it wasn't the steaks causing her to drool. It was *him*. The solid, sturdy build, the thick dark hair she'd recently run her fingers through. A flash of the sexy night they'd spent together fired every last one of her cylinders. Him sliding deep inside her, those dark eyes fastened on hers… "Hungry?"

She blinked him into focus and lifted one eyebrow. "Starving." She didn't mean for dinner and held his gaze long enough to communicate as much. Vic offered a sideways smirk, but it died the second Eddie stepped into the house.

"Let's eat," Eddie said.

Dinner was blessedly uneventful, with small talk about anything and everything *not* having to do with Vic or Aubrey. Dad talked about sports and Mom about her book club. When the topic of the Texas Cattleman's Club pool party came up, her father quickly changed the subject. Aubrey didn't have the foggiest memory of the chili cook-off.

"Was the winner announced or did I ruin the contest?" she'd asked. The table had fallen silent, the scraping of knives and forks on plates halting at her question. "Who has the best chili in Royal, Texas, anyway?" She'd taken a bite of her steak and chewed, preferring to treat this odd circumstance as run-of-the-mill, but she hadn't received an answer.

"This is very frustrating," she told Vic now. They'd finished their dinners, and her mother had refused her offer to help with the dishes.

Aubrey and Vic walked down the long, winding driveway side by side, the crunching of gravel underfoot interspersed with crickets sawing away in the tall grass. "I don't see why no one can give me a summary of events."

"Are you a doctor now?" Vic came to a halt and faced her, his silhouette grainy in the dark and backlit by the moon. Even in low light, he was the most handsome man she'd ever laid eyes on. "Patience used to be a strong suit of yours, Aub."

"I want to remember. I *need* to remember."

"You will," he said with enough authority that she believed him. As if her amnesia was nothing more than a blip on the radar of an otherwise normal life. That soon she'd be driving, playing brightly colored games on her cell phone and returning to work. She missed her normal life. She loved teaching more than anything, and not having the comfort of her routine—even one she couldn't remember every detail of—was difficult.

He started walking again, bypassing his truck rather than climbing into it. She was fine with prolonging the evening, though she wished they had more privacy. Dad was probably peeking out the window at them right now.

Vic clasped her hand, and she wove her fingers with his, the warmth of his touch going a long way to making her feel better. "Enjoy the moment. That's all you have to do. Live your life until your memory returns."

"I have one *very* vivid memory of us from the other night." She squeezed his hand.

"Oh yeah?"

"Mmm-hmm. The night before my accident. My bedroom. You taking my clothes off and running your tongue over every part of my body. You were starved for me, Vic, like it was the last time we'd be together. It was hot."

She didn't miss when his arm stiffened against hers.

"Don't worry, we're far enough from the house they can't hear. I don't understand why we couldn't lie and say we're going out for ice cream and then sneak into my apartment for a quickie, do you?" She certainly wasn't incapable of physical affection. She could walk, talk, recite her favorite Walt Whitman poem. She was missing a few measly pieces from her past, that was all.

"Sex is, not, um…" Vic swiped his brow, looking uncharacteristically nervous. He wasn't shy. Not at all. He knew what she liked and delivered each and every time. Well, the times she could remember. "Your health is more important."

"Sex is very healthy." She leaned against his arm, relieved to hear his soft laugh in the dark.

"I know, honey. It does us a world of good. But I beg of you, stop reminding me what I'm missing out on when I'm trying to be noble."

"Nobility from Vic Grandin." She sighed, defeated. "I don't like it."

His grin literally weakened her knees. She clutched his hand tighter. What she wouldn't give to have him naked and next to her tonight. "Can I at least have a kiss?"

"When did you turn into a siren?"

"I don't recall you complaining in the past."

"Ain't that the problem?" Proud of his quip, he winked. She balled her fist and socked his shoulder.

"All right, all right." He tipped his head to the side. "One kiss, but then you have to let me go home. Your daddy's watching."

She wanted to say she didn't care if God himself was watching, but she decided not to press her luck. She wasn't as fragile as everyone thought she was, but she could also admit that she didn't know what she didn't know. Hell, for what little she remembered, she could be a Russian spy with a death toll that rivaled that of a seasoned hit man instead of a hometown teacher.

"I'm not a Russian spy, am I?"

"What?" He laughed the word, his breath coasting over her lips. She tipped her chin in anticipation.

"Nothing." She was going to have to trust the people who loved her for a while. She could live with that.

He closed the gap and touched his lips to hers. They hovered there, mouths moving, arms touching, fingers intertwined. He cradled her head and deepened the kiss, a gentle slide of his tongue on hers, polite but completely mind-altering. The slower he went, the more he savored the kiss, the more she wanted him. Impatient, she speared her tongue into his mouth, yanking the front of his shirt in an effort to get closer to him. Their bodies bumped, her belly encountering hardness behind the fly of his jeans. *Yes, yes, yes.* This was what she wanted. To feel what he felt for her. To have him again and feel a modicum of normalcy in a completely abnormal situation.

He sucked in a sharp inhale. She lost his lips, and the rest of him, her breasts brushing his chest as he pulled away. His expression was playful but scolding when he took a literal step away from her and shoved his hands deep in his pockets. With a shake of his head, he said, "You always knew how to make me forget my place, Ms. Collins."

"I guess we have that in common, Mr. Grandin."

She spun on her heel to head back to the house, along the way trying to decide if she was more disappointed or flattered by his words.

Five

Vic arrived at his office in the Grandin family home the next morning and was immediately surrounded by his two older sisters. Chelsea and Layla were standing, arms folded, foreheads creased.

"What'd I do now?" He moved to the coffee cart on the back wall, relieved someone had been saintly enough to brew a pot before he'd arrived. He'd had a virtually sleepless night after the kiss Aubrey had given him in her parents' driveway.

The old Vic would have thrown her into his truck and left a cloud of dust in his wake as he raced her to his bedroom. Once there, he would have finished what she'd so brazenly started. But since the night he'd recently spent with her, he'd realized he'd been a selfish ass for way too long. Add to that her compromised memory and his starring role as her white knight and there was no way he could act on his impulses. If not for a sudden attack of conscience, he could've spent last night making love to her on every sturdy surface in his room instead of lying on his back, wide-awake, with a hard-on that wouldn't quit.

Being mature sucked.

"You didn't *do* anything." Layla sounded sincere. Her wavy blond hair was down, her mouth set in a determined line. The look was uncommon given she'd been happier lately. Ever since she'd fallen in love with and married Josh.

"We're here for the quarterly meeting, as per Daddy's request," Chelsea said.

Shit. He'd totally forgotten. His head had been elsewhere last night. On the faint freckles dotting the bridge of Aubrey's nose, and the feel of her tight little fist clutching his shirt. She'd wanted him, and he'd refused her. God, he was a jackass.

"Well, where is he?" Vic sipped his coffee as he glanced out of the office window at the stables. No sign of his father anywhere.

"We thought you would know, you two being so close and all," Chelsea answered with a smirk. Vic refused to take the bait. He didn't have the energy to argue with her today.

"I'll saddle up Titan and find him." Cell reception was spotty in many areas of their expansive ranch.

On the back of his gray roan Percheron, Vic rode the perimeter of the ranch in search of Victor Jr. No sign of his father's horse, or his wide black cowboy hat, but he did spot a woman at the edge of the

Grandin property, right where it butted up against Lattimore land.

"Help you?" he called out as he approached the stranger. Her hand rested on the hilt of a measuring wheel. "You're a surveyor."

"How'd you know?" A quick lift of her eyebrows told him she was surprised to see him, but she hid it with a smile. "Was it the measuring device or my bright orange safety vest that tipped you off?"

The woman was both tall and slender, wearing a flannel beneath that safety vest paired with jeans and boots. The way she looked him dead in the eye suggested she wasn't the least bit intimidated.

"This is private property."

"No worries. I'm done here," she answered.

"What *were* you doing here?" He didn't expect an answer, but once again she addressed him directly.

"I was hired."

"By who?"

"By whom, you mean, and the answer is Heath Thurston."

Heath. Of course. That bastard was getting bolder by the minute. The reminder that Thurston was still trying to wrap his grubby paws around the deeds to the Grandin and Lattimore ranches made Vic see red.

"Have a good day now. That's a beautiful horse." With a flip of her blond hair, the slight woman made her way to the road with her equipment in tow. Vic made sure she was gone before heading back to the house himself.

On his way he encountered Layla, who was riding a fairly cooperative mustang today. She trained horses, so she knew what she was doing, which was why she'd soon be opening her own ranch with Josh. Vic felt the odd pinch of loss that she'd be here at the family ranch less and less…so long as they could hold on to it.

The mustang grumbled his complaint but came into line as Layla walked him next to Vic and Titan on the way to the house.

"Who was that?" she asked.

"A surveyor hired by Heath Thurston."

"Damn," his sister said under her breath.

"Yeah, I know."

"How do you know she was sent by Heath?"

"She told me. Apparently no one is being shy about the land they want to take from us and the Lattimores."

"We have what everyone wants, Vic. Look around."

He took in the blue skies and the ranch land dotted with cows of all colors. Utopia. A utopia they could lose if Heath Thurston continued to press the issue of oil rights. The other man saw it as his way of righting the scales. His deceased mother and half sister weren't here to fight for the land they were presumably promised, so Heath was doing it for them. Heath's twin brother, Chelsea's fiancé, Nolan, had decided to remain neutral.

Vic didn't buy it.

He'd never admit to his sisters how much the threat scared him, or how close this litigation was coming to causing a serious kink in his family's and the Lattimores' lives. Vic cared about this ranch, beyond running it for his pride's sake. This was his family home. He refused to lose it.

"The Grandins and the Lattimores have been neighbors for as long as anyone can remember." He squinted up at the bright blue sky covering their lands and beyond. "Can you imagine if—"

"No," Layla interrupted. "I'm not going to imagine what if." Her eyes were as hard as steel, but he saw fear behind them. He'd do anything to protect his sisters from what was going on right under their noses. He felt so damned helpless in this situation. "I might be building a life of my own, but the Grandin ranch will always be home."

They dismounted at the barn, leaving their horses to be cared for by the stable hands, before they walked back toward the house.

"I'm heading back to my ranch to see how the construction is going. If you spot Daddy, send my regrets on missing the meeting." Layla slapped Vic's shoulder and wandered off in the direction of her car.

Some days the idea of everything resting on his shoulders wasn't as romantic a notion as it had been when he was younger. He'd imagined wielding both power and control like his father, with a fair hand. Vic had prided himself on being firm and decisive, but now that he was older, he saw how many situations were not simply black and white. There were as many shades of gray as on his horse Titan, and those shades often bled together, making for a muddy canvas. Individual colors were impossible to distinguish.

That made him think of Aubrey. There was no black-and-white way of thinking with her, and she'd muddied his mind more than anything. When he'd gone to dinner last night, he'd resolved not to kiss her. He'd changed his mind the moment she'd followed him outside. One look into her jade-green eyes and he hadn't been able to tell her no. Not when she'd looked at him like she still loved him. Which, he supposed, she thought she still did.

He scrubbed his forehead and sighed, the day feeling long already, and it'd only just begun. When he stepped back into his office, his coffee had gone cold and his father was sitting at Vic's desk.

"You're late. Layla and Chelsea have gone."

"You're the one taking over, son." His father shrugged.

Hell, here they went again.

By the time the sun was setting, Vic was well and truly beat. He needed sleep, or at least to destress. Typically he'd call Jayden so they could go out, but the question was *go out and do what?*

Drink beer? Flirt with women? Not only did Vic not want to flirt with other women, but he was practically betrothed now that he was pretending to Aubrey they'd never split. He didn't mind as much as he thought he would have. For the last ten years, he'd been judicious about the women he dated, so he hadn't made any future plans. A future with a woman was something he'd only imagined with Aubrey, back when she'd worn the engagement ring he'd put on her finger.

He'd slipped right back into that mode of thinking. It was like they'd stepped into a time machine and had traveled back to high school. The hand-holding, the kisses in her parents' driveway, denying each other the sex they so desperately wanted... He'd held out for a little over two years before he and Aubrey slept together. Her first time. His first time. He wasn't typically sentimental, but thinking back on those days caused his chest to constrict. They'd lost so much, which made for an odd parallel to potentially losing the family ranch.

Without overthinking it, he picked up the phone and called her. When her sweet voice answered, he said, "About that ice cream you wanted..."

Thirty minutes later he and Aubrey were sitting outside Dairy Prairie, a new ice-cream shop in Royal. He'd gone with a scoop of rocky road on a waffle cone, while Aubrey had opted for double-chocolate macadamia nut on a wafer cone. Having licked her way down to the base of the cone, she took her first bite. At least the torture part of the evening was over for him. Watching her pink tongue lap away at the sweet cream had sent his brain free-falling into the gutter.

"Doesn't that taste like Styrofoam?" he asked before taking a bite of his waffle cone. Crisp, sugary deliciousness. "Wafer cones are tragic."

"I like wafer cones." She shoved him, rolling her eyes playfully. He soaked up the moment. He'd learned the hard way to treasure her not looking at him like he was a horrible person. "How was your day at the ranch?"

The stress he'd been successfully avoiding rolled back in like the tide. "Peachy."

"And your sisters?"

"Oh, you know. Chelsea is engaged to Nolan Thurston. Layla is married to Joshua Banks. Morgan is single and maintaining her role as everyone's favorite Grandin." Just the facts. He didn't know how much Aubrey knew, or what she remembered.

"Married, wow. Did I forget the wedding?" Her lips pulled into a small frown.

"No. We didn't go. They were married in Vegas."

She took a moment to digest that news, then tilted her head. "Is this where you wait for me to argue that *you're* my favorite Grandin?"

"Definitely not," he answered honestly. "Morgan's my favorite, so if you chose her, I'd understand."

"I know you and Chelsea have always been at odds, but at her core she wants what's best for the family."

Like for him to stay away from Aubrey? He wouldn't tell her about Chels's miniature tirade yesterday. It'd hurt Aubrey's feelings. Plus, Chelsea was wrong. He wasn't causing any harm sitting on a bench outside an ice-cream shop and talking with Aubrey. Hell, he was *helping*. Being with her was as good a destressor as any. No, the best. Which was likely why he let his guard down and bitched about his day rather than carefully tiptoeing around what was happening with his family. He'd never held back with Aubrey and didn't much care for it now.

As they finished eating their ice-cream cones, he shared about coming across the surveyor, who he'd learned from his father was named Ruby Rose Bennett. She'd been hired to poke around on the Grandin and Lattimore land in search of actual oil beneath it. "Heath is trying to carve out a piece for his family, but what he doesn't realize is there are other families he could destroy in the process."

Aubrey slipped her palm into his and wove their fingers together. The weight of her hand in his and the other resting on his biceps took his anxiety down a few more notches. "It's awful someone's threatening your ranch. I can't imagine the tension it's causing both your family and the Lattimores."

Always thinking of everyone else, that was his Aubrey. She wasn't *his*, per se, but they were overlooking that inconvenient fact for the moment.

"Chelsea and I have always butted heads, you're right about that. But not on this topic. She and Nolan have agreed to be neutral parties and let the legal battle play out without a fight."

"Wow."

"Yeah." Vic's laugh was dark. "Don't be fooled. She has plenty of fight left in her."

"You mean over who inherits the ranch," Aubrey said, proving she'd retained quite a bit of memories from when they were younger.

"Chels has always believed she should be in charge because she's firstborn."

Aubrey hummed in thought.

"What?" he asked, unable to stand the suspense.

"Do you think it's fair?"

"That Chelsea gives me hell when it wasn't my decision to run the ranch in the first place? No, I don't."

"No. Do you think it's fair that Chelsea was passed over simply because you're a man?"

He opened his mouth to argue, but rather than trot out a defense about how it was not only fair, but also deserved since he'd worked damn hard at the ranch, he paused. The fact was Chelsea worked damn hard, too. She always had. Vic hadn't seen the ranch issue from Chelsea's point of view very often over the years, if at all. He'd been too busy smugly declaring how he'd been handpicked by his father and grandfather to be in charge.

Damn. That'd been the same guy who had pushed Aubrey away. Was it any wonder she left and never turned back?

"What if you and your sisters ran the ranch together?"

"Ha!" His grin faded fast when Aubrey regarded him sincerely.

"Sharing responsibilities is a plausible compromise, Vic. The three of you are smart and care deeply about the family ranch. No one would work harder to keep it running for generations to come."

"If we can't stop these interlopers, there won't be a ranch to fight over, Aub. If there's oil on the land, they'll destroy every inch of it searching for black gold."

"All the more reason for the Grandin siblings to work together."

He'd always loved her sweetness, but he hadn't always appreciated her pragmatism. He placed his free hand over hers in a show of appreciation. The idea of a compromise with his sisters, especially Chelsea, used to seem like defeat to him. Young Vic would have sooner died than admit his oldest, bossiest sister was right. Admittedly, there was a version of him that still didn't want to cede control over what was destined to be his. Then again, hadn't he been thinking earlier today how stressful it was to handle everything on his own? Losing the ranch was too steep a price to pay to preserve his pride.

"You're right," he said.

Aubrey gasped, clutching her chest as if she were having a heart attack. "Did Vic Grandin admit that I was *right*?"

"Stop it," he told her when she drew the attention of surrounding patrons with the mini scene she was making.

"Look forward to an end to this heat wave, folks," she announced to no one in particular. "Hell has frozen over!"

She opened her mouth—to say what else, he had no idea—so he leaned in and stamped a hard kiss onto her parted lips. She softened beneath him, and a hum worked its way up her throat, where it reverberated against his lips.

It was heaven.

Kiss complete, she folded her arms and did her best to look inconvenienced. "You win this round, Vic."

But she wasn't inconvenienced. He could see how much she'd enjoyed that kiss by the blush staining her cheeks.

Six

"I'm not sure this is a good idea," Aubrey's mother said for the eighteenth time, or was it for the *eightieth* time?

"Yes, you've made that clear." Aubrey swiped shiny lip gloss onto her mouth and, satisfied with her reflection, turned to her mother and held out both arms. "What do you think?"

"You're so beautiful it's hard to believe you came from me."

"You're still a fox from head to toe, Mary Collins. Never let anyone tell you differently." Aubrey fiddled with her naked fingers. "Did you pack any of my jewelry when you went to my apartment? I'd love a ring or a necklace." All she had with her were the diamond stud earrings she'd been wearing the night of the cook-off.

"I didn't think to grab any, but I do have a Christmas gift socked away for you."

Aubrey pressed her palms together. She loved nothing more than Christmas, unless it was early Christmas presents. "I beg of you. I'll never ask for another thing again if you give it to me today."

"Some things never change." In her bedroom, Mary pulled open a drawer in her jewelry chest and plucked out a blue Tiffany & Co. box.

"Mom." Aubrey stared, overwhelmed. Her mother had bought her nice gifts before, but a piece of jewelry from Tiffany was far from the norm. "This feels special. Unless I'm forgetting a few years' worth of extravagant gifts?"

"No," her mother said. "You are not forgetting. Your father and I had a very good year with our investments, and we're treating our daughter."

Aubrey opened the box top to reveal a delicate gold chain with a key pendant. In the center of the key was a diamond. "It's…wow, so beautiful."

"You'll always have a home with us, no matter where life takes you. I bought it before your accident, but the sentiment is more apt now. Since you've been temporarily displaced." Her mother hooked the necklace around Aubrey's neck and turned her to face the full-length mirror.

Last night, Vic had called her and asked if she wanted to go out to a nice dinner. Aubrey had nearly leaped for joy. Dinner at her parents' house and a trip to an ice-cream shop were nice, but she wanted to have a *real* date with him. Preferably one that ended in his bedroom, which she fully intended to talk him into as soon as possible.

That morning, in preparation, she'd taken a Lyft to Saint Tropez Salon for a trim. With her auburn hair styled in luscious waves, she'd then popped into the Rancher's Daughter for something to wear tonight. Morgan had been behind the counter and had helped Aubrey pick out a stunning siren-red A-line dress. The skirt was knee-length and swishy, the sleeves missing, perfect to display her toned arms. At Morgan's further insistence, Aubrey had also purchased a sexy, strappy pair of shoes—with low heels, since spindly ones weren't a challenge she needed. The necklace from her mother pulled the entire look together.

"It's perfect. Thank you, Mom." She hugged her mother tight. When she let go, she noticed the worry lines etched into Mary's brow anew. "Don't start. He's taking me dancing, not stock-car racing."

"At least you took a car into town rather than drive yourself."

"See? I listen sometimes." Aubrey smiled.

"When you fell, you weren't doing anything remotely dangerous. How can I be sure you're safe out there?"

"I'll be on level ground, and I'll be with Vic. I'm in the best, most capable hands."

Twenty minutes later, Aubrey opened her mother's front door to find Vic beneath the covered porch. He wore a dark pair of jeans and boots, a collared shirt and a sport jacket. His shirt beneath was open at the collar, giving her a peek at the tanned column of his throat. And the way the jacket showcased his broad shoulders was nearly too much to process.

"Aubrey. God, you look beautiful." His awestruck expression sent droves of goose bumps down her arms.

"Do you like it?" She held out the skirt and did a quarter turn. "Morgan helped me pick it out."

"Hell yeah, I like it." His cunning smile appeared, making her wish they could skip dinner and go straight to him taking this dress off her.

"What time are you coming home, gingerbread?" her father interrupted—on purpose—from his recliner in the living room.

"I don't know," she called back, unable to mask her frustration. To Vic, she said, "They treat me like I'm a teenager."

"We do not," Mary chimed in, sneaking up on her. "We are treating you like you have an injury. You shouldn't press your luck."

"I won't let her out of my sight," Vic vowed, but his eyes never left Aubrey's.

The short drive landed them at the valet station of Sheen, a restaurant constructed almost entirely of glass. She'd wanted to try it the moment she'd heard about it. When Vic had mentioned the restaurant, she'd carefully asked if he'd ever taken her there and he'd said no. "It'll be the first time for both of us."

He offered his arm and walked them inside. The hostess swiftly seated them at the rear of the dining room, where a candlelit table for two was shrouded in shadows. Aubrey gawped at the kitchen, in full view in the center of the restaurant. What a unique and modern atmosphere.

He pulled out her chair for her and ordered a bottle of something she'd never heard of before. "What was that?"

"Chardonnay. Unless you'd like a martini?"

She cringed. "No. I won't be having another of those."

"I thought martinis were your thing?"

"I don't know what made me order one at the Silver Saddle, but I distinctly remember not liking it."

He seemed contemplative about her admission but said no more about it.

She lifted the heavy, leather-bound menu, taking her time reading each mouthwatering description. "What do I choose?"

"Anything you like," he responded easily. "We're celebrating."

"What are we celebrating?"

"You. Me. Isn't that enough?"

"You mentioned dancing?" She swept her eyes over the dining room. There was no dance floor, unless he intended to hop onto the tabletop.

"Not here. Across the street at the botanical gardens. They have an outdoor tent, and afterward, we can visit the butterfly garden."

"I love that garden." She knew that on an intuitive level, at least. She could call up a picture of the lush green setting and multicolored wings fluttering around her. "You must have taken me before."

His smile faltered. "Not me. You went with friends, I think."

"Oh. Right." It was so odd not being able to place him in the memories she did have. It was like he'd been erased from some of them.

"Are you feeling okay?"

"I guess so. It's odd how I recall some things but others are blank. I can't explain it. Why can't I remember you? You're the most important person in my life. You should be there." Her heart burned with unspent emotions—frustration, worry, fear.

He reached over the table to take her hand, giving her fingers a squeeze. "None of that matters tonight, Aub. We'll make as many new memories as we can until the old ones return."

She swallowed back the tears that threatened. "If they return."

"When they return," he corrected.

"I miss my apartment," she admitted with a weak smile. "How do you live in your family's home without losing your mind?"

"We're not exactly on top of each other at the ranch. Morg and I practically have our own wings. Layla and Josh are living in a hotel while their ranch house is being built. Chels is staying with her fiancé. The house is emptier than it's ever been."

"Intriguing." She hoisted a teasing eyebrow.

His eyes darkened with intent, but he didn't speak.

The sommelier delivered their wine, allowing her to taste first. It was buttery and smooth, the perfect chardonnay. When they were alone again, Vic raised his wineglass in a toast.

"To new and lasting memories."

She'd drink to that.

* * *

Vic sipped his wine and watched the beautiful woman across from him at the table. She was exquisite and, for tonight, his. He was playing with fire by bringing her out for a romantic date, but a plan had hatched and hadn't let go of him yet.

If he could make enough good memories with Aubrey during his time with her, then when her memory fully returned, the good would far outweigh the bad.

In theory.

He wasn't sure of that, or really anything anymore. His foundation was less bedrock than shifting sands in an hourglass. His recent crisis of character had cropped up when he'd stepped in to play the role of Aubrey's boyfriend. Admitting to her that he'd been shortsighted when it'd come to him inheriting the ranch had shaken him further.

In the past, plenty of people had written him off as arrogant and entitled. A role he'd played to perfection. Growing up, his father and grandfather had never given Vic any reason to believe he wasn't 100 percent worthy of the good things in life coming his way. Which was probably why he'd behaved like a self-consumed prick. He'd taken Aubrey for granted back then. In his mind, there was simply no way she would walk away from him. He'd seen himself as the ultimate catch. Husband material, through and through.

With ten years of dirty water under the bridge between them, it would take a lot to convince her he'd changed for the better. Ironically, if it wasn't for her accident, he could kiss the idea of this reunion goodbye. He might have been able to talk her back into bed with him, but her guard had been up that night after the Silver Saddle. Chances were good she'd never have considered him as anything more than a bed buddy.

Back when they'd split up, he'd been shocked when she'd thrown the engagement ring at him. He'd been an arrogant teen who'd grown into an arrogant twenty-one-year-old. Things always went his way—and if they didn't, he got off with a warning. Speeding tickets, a brush with the law for underage drinking at a party, sneaking into his neighbor's backyard and using the pool… Vic had been let off the hook more times than he could count. His family name afforded him privilege, but Aubrey was a privilege he didn't appreciate until she was long gone.

Their final argument as an engaged couple had been venomous and heated, the venom coming mostly, if not completely, from his side. The conversation had started off innocently, with her mentioning grad school. When she'd skipped off to college, he hadn't seen enough of her. He couldn't wrap his head around *more* years without her. Her priority had become studying and not him, and he hadn't liked it one bit. When she'd mentioned wanting to continue her education, he'd been completely ungracious.

"Graduate school? What the hell for? You'll be my wife, Aub. A pampered woman, a mother to my children. What more could you want?"

He flinched now as he thought back to what a selfish asshole he'd been. In his desperation to keep her close, he'd done the complete opposite. He'd pushed her so far away, she'd seen no other option than to leave him permanently. He guzzled down the rest of his glass of wine before refilling it from the bottle on the table.

"More stress at the ranch?" Aubrey asked. Their shrimp bruschetta arrived, and he lifted a strip of candied bacon off the top and gnawed on it. He figured it wasn't a lie to say yes.

"Yes, but nothing I can't handle."

"I'm not surprised. You've always excelled at your job."

Humbled by the compliment, he redirected to her. "You're one to talk, teacher of the year. I'm proud of you."

"Thank you." The wistfulness in her smile was genuine, but her smile faded when she added, "I miss work. I was just getting to know my students. When I sent my lesson plans to the substitute taking my place, it was like handing someone my firstborn. I'm itching to go back and do it myself. Immediately after typing up that email, though, I had a headache behind my eyes. I'm beginning to worry I'll never be normal."

He reached across the table and took her hand again, regretting that he wasn't on the same side of the table so he could hug her close while he reassured her. He realized it wasn't his place, but he couldn't help standing up for the woman she was—the woman she would be again. "Listen to me, Aubrey. You will recover and be more of a force to reckon with than you were before. You always knew what you wanted, and you were strong enough to say it."

"Well, guess what, Vic? I want more than to be your little wife and pop out your babies. I have

dreams, too. I want to achieve things in my life that have nothing to do with you. I know that's hard to believe, seeing as how your future's been preplanned from birth, but the ranch is not my dream. The world doesn't stop and start on your command, and neither will I."

"Is it any wonder why I love you?" Her current wide-eyed admiration was at odds with the fiery speech she'd given him before she'd ended them forever.

He knew she meant the *I love you*—at least, some part of her did—but he couldn't reconcile that love with their tumultuous breakup. It was embedded so deeply in his hippocampus, he doubted even a knock to the head would erase it completely.

Seven

The Royal Discovery Botanical Gardens were made up of, according to the welcome sign, "8 Acres of Land Serving as a Texas Oasis."

There was a massive white tent furnished with outdoor air conditioners. On their way to the tent, they approached a round decorative fountain. Aubrey, her hand in Vic's, stared down into the splashing water where pennies to buy wishes had been tossed, and she wondered what they represented. Love? Money? Memory recovery?

"Penny for your thoughts?" Vic waggled her hand when she didn't answer right away.

"I have an embarrassing question," she finally mustered the courage to say. She looked up at his handsome, questioning face. "Why don't we live together? I'm sure there's a plausible reason, but I can't remember it."

Them living apart made no sense. They'd been dating since high school and were in love with each other, and yet he lived on the ranch with his family and she had her own place. Funds weren't a problem for Vic, and she had a healthy bank account as well. Why hadn't they purchased a slice of land to call their own by now? The answer seemed just out of reach.

"Aubrey…"

Frustrated by his tone, which hinted he might blow her off instead of give her an answer, she held up a palm. "Please don't tell me you're trying to protect me by not telling me why."

"Okay." He inhaled deeply, pausing to glance over his shoulder at the tent where ticketed couples were entering. He was probably wishing he'd taken her inside to dance rather than lingering at the Contemplate Your Life fountain. Finally, he turned back to her. "You were prioritizing graduate school when we were trying to decide on a future. We haven't spoken about it since."

"At all?"

"Not a word." He held her gaze steadily. He wasn't lying. She could tell.

Graduate school. The mere mention of those two words sparked…well, not a memory, but a feeling. She'd passionately pursued school and had made education her priority. Had she prioritized her career over Vic? It didn't paint a pretty picture of her former self.

"It was the right thing to do," he said. "My future

was laid out for me, so at the time I didn't understand your drive to go to school and have a career separate from what I could provide. I was wrong, which you told me. Then you proved it to me. You achieved exactly what you set out to do, Ms. Collins."

"And it ultimately didn't hurt our relationship." Her hand in his, she noted the stiffness in his fingers as well as his answering silence. No matter what arguments must have ensued around that very topic, they were here, together. She hadn't blown him off to date a frat boy or given up on them. She'd instinctively known Vic was the best man for her.

"Would you like to go inside?" he invited.

"I didn't wear my dancing shoes for nothing."

"Slow songs only. Doctor's orders."

Lights were strung and a twinkling chandelier hung from the center of the tent. A four-piece band on a stage played sophisticated, smooth jazz. Perfect for slow dancing.

Couples of all ages were either sitting at the sparse round tables enjoying sparkling cocktails or swaying to the music on a parquet dance floor atop the manicured lawn. Potted plants, in a variety of sizes from tall to stout, were arranged in the corners, small engraved signs announcing the genus and species jabbed into the soil.

"Not only an entertaining evening, but an educational one as well," she said as she stroked a particularly broad Monstera leaf.

"I thought you'd appreciate that. Do you want a drink?"

She shook her head.

"How about a dance?"

"That I'll take."

Nothing felt more right than joining Vic on the dance floor. They fell into sync with each other as they moved to the music, her hand in his as he held her close. Dancing with him while wearing a beautiful dress sparked a memory from their past—more clear and crisp than any she'd had since the accident. She laughed aloud, so thrilled to have it shining bright for her to observe.

He smiled with her. "What is it?"

"A memory. It came out of nowhere and now here it is, crystal clear. Prom. My senior prom." She arched an eyebrow. "I wore red."

"Everywhere," he growled against the tender shell of her ear. "From a lacy bra and panty set to the dress with no sleeves. Not a single spaghetti strap to save me."

"Nope. Nothing but cleavage for days, and I wore a push-up bra. I was on a mission." She'd planned the perfect night—she'd vowed to lose her virginity to Vic on prom night. He'd been patient. She'd been patient, though they'd had plenty of make-out nights at his family's house or hers that had nearly trampled over that line drawn in the sand. If she was anything, it was decisive. She'd known what she wanted and had refused to let anyone talk her into—or out of—sleeping with him.

"We couldn't be stopped," she whispered, butterflies of excitement fluttering in her stomach. "And now here we are, roadblocks everywhere."

"Tell me more about prom. Since you so keenly recall the circumstances of the evening."

"You mean you don't?"

"Oh, I remember." His lips hovered over hers, his breath warm against her mouth. "I remember every last hitched breath and honey-sweet taste." He backed away, taking some of her focus off the past and placing it squarely in the present. "I want your take on it."

"It was a lot like tonight." She rested her other hand on his shoulder and squeezed. "You kept promising to treat me well after we left the dance. I was nervous, and you were totally collected."

"I was not." He chuckled, his grin both boyish and charming. "I was scared to death I'd screw up and you'd hate it and never touch me again."

"You were?" How had she not known? "Confident, capable Vic Grandin?"

"I didn't want to disappoint you."

His sincerity was an arrow to her heart. She wrapped both arms around his neck and held him close. "You didn't disappoint me."

"No, I didn't. But there was a power shift that night." He led her into a smooth turn. She followed, finding it easy to trust him. "You could get me to do that anytime you wanted."

"What about now? You don't seem as easily convinced."

He kept his smile, and he didn't tell her no. Maybe she was getting somewhere.

"We've been seeing each other, but we haven't seen *enough* of each other, if you catch my meaning."

He angled his head, those dark eyes sparkling

with thoughts he wasn't sharing. He'd caught her meaning, all right. She toyed with his hair, scraping her fingernails upward. A slight shake spanned the width of his shoulders. Yes, she was far from powerless when it came to Vic. He was as weak for her as she was for him.

"It's been a couple weeks since we rolled around in bed together. We're due. Don't tell me you don't want me, too. I can see it."

"You can feel it, too." He grabbed her hips and bumped his pelvis against her. A hard, unyielding part of him had definitely received the sex memo and was on board.

His gaze slid to the side, presumably to check if anyone was watching them—they weren't. "You have talked me right into trouble. I hope you're proud of yourself."

She beamed up at him. She was, actually.

"Stay here with me for a song or two so I can calm down, and, I beg of you, talk about *anything* else."

"Anything?"

"Anything not sexy." He raised an eyebrow.

"You're no fun in your old age. I recall you eagerly sliding the hotel key card into the door and tearing my prom dress in your haste to have me naked."

"Yeah, well, what you don't know is how hard it was for me to last longer than getting you naked took," he said, and she had to laugh.

It wasn't like him to be self-deprecating. He wore it well, though the expression of chagrin faded into one of complete and utter confidence in a blink. That long-ago night, he had lasted a lot longer than he'd jokingly stated. She'd been ready to go again shortly after, and so they had. The lie she'd told her parents about them going to a friend's party after the dance was easy to justify. She was in love. Vic was the only one for her. What better way to spend her prom night than in his arms?

She'd been an hour and a half late for her 2:00 a.m. curfew, but her mother hadn't been upset. Dad had been another story, but her mom refused to let him stay angry. "We were young once, too, Eddie," Mary had reminded him.

"Those were the good ole days," Vic said, sounding oddly solemn. "We didn't know it back then."

"*Hello.* We're not dead yet. We have plenty of good days left. If you'd let yourself have a little fun." She poked him in the center of the chest and waited for him to laugh and agree. He didn't.

"There are times you're not remembering, Aubrey." Pain bloomed in his brown eyes. "All couples argue. You don't remember the bad times."

"I don't remember many times, bad or good," she amended. "But I know what feels right. This feels right. Being apart, even for a few days, feels wrong. I understand why we chose to live separately initially, but it doesn't make sense to me now. No matter what memories return about us arguing over where to eat for dinner or who should drive to the restaurant, I can't imagine not wanting you." His heart pounded, strong and sure, against her palm. "I'm not as fragile as my doctor and my parents believe. I'm here, Vic. All of me. That fall didn't change the core of who I am."

He stopped moving, standing still in the middle of the dance floor, his eyes drilling into hers as other couples swished around them in a blur.

"I hope with everything I am, Aubrey Collins," he said, his lips hovering over hers, "that you're right."

"I'm right," she promised, leaning up for a kiss he returned. As his mouth moved over hers, she lost herself in the moment. A beautiful moment she promised to remember until her dying day.

Eight

"We're cooking tonight," Layla announced as she strolled through the open doors of the barn. "Josh and I. We'd like you to bring Aubrey to dinner with you."

Vic had come in here to think, and he did his best thinking while riding Titan. Now saddled up, the gray speckled horse was itching to go out and run, and so was Vic.

"You're cooking?"

"Yes. Here at the house, obviously, since Josh and I don't have one yet. The staff has the night off, so the timing is perfect."

Like he'd told Aubrey, Layla and Josh had been living at the hotel until their new house was built. They didn't exactly relish the idea of living here as newlyweds, which he understood. But dinner? That was new.

"Why?"

"Why?" She blinked at him, waited and then filled the gap when she determined he had no more to say. "I'd like to use the gourmet kitchen at the house to practice. We won't have a cook like Mom and Dad do, at least not right away. And you eat too many cheeseburgers."

"Do not," he argued, but she wasn't wrong. He led Titan from the barn into the sunshine-filled day. "Bringing Aubrey to dinner isn't a good idea, Lay."

"Why not?" His sister followed him outside. "Afraid she'll remember what actually happened between you two?"

After the kiss they'd shared, and Aubrey practically begging him to take her to bed, yeah, one could say he wasn't eager for the bad memories to come flooding back.

"I ran into her at Morgan's shop in town the other day," Layla said. "She mentioned we don't see enough of each other. What was I supposed to do? Blow her off?"

"Yes." Titan snuffled his agreement. "You could have blown her off. Or you could've invited her to coffee that day. Not invite her here, to ground zero."

He gestured to their family home, the massive Western-style structure a hulking behemoth against azure skies. Aubrey had thrown the engagement ring at him in this very driveway.

"You can't keep her from remembering," Layla said gently. "It's the best thing for her."

"I know." But was it so wrong to want this part to last awhile longer? He wasn't ready to let go of the Aubrey who beamed up at him while reminding him how they'd lost their virginity to each other long ago. It was hard not to delay the inevitable. "It's just you and Josh?"

"And Chelsea." Layla wouldn't meet his eyes when she added, "And Nolan."

"Nolan?"

"His twin brother isn't anyone's favorite person, but Nolan is not Heath. Nolan is also with Chelsea, so you'd better get used to it."

"At least tell me Morgan is coming."

"Nope. She's doing inventory tonight, and Mom, Dad and Grandma are eating at the Lattimores'. Barbara is showcasing her recipes from her upcoming cookbook."

"A family dinner wasn't the circumstance under which I pictured bringing Aubrey back to the ranch for the first time in years," he grumbled.

"Come on, baby brother. Aubrey loves us." Layla swatted his hat off his head. He caught it before it hit the dirt—barely.

He hated when his older sister talked to him like he was a kid, especially when she followed it up with the hat thing she'd done way too often when they *were* kids.

"You can't say anything to Aubrey to jog her memory. She believes we're together, and her doctor thinks it's best if she comes to any other conclusions on her own."

"No one will blow your cover. Chels and I would

never do anything to disrupt her healing. Tell me you know that."

He knew that, but he didn't answer. Worry was writhing in his stomach at the idea of Aubrey being here. In this house. Would she remember their horrible fight from years ago?

"She's not allowed to work right now, which means she's not seeing her friends. She has her parents and she has you. She needs a bigger support system than that. We all do."

Dammit. He didn't like when Layla was right—when either of his older sisters were right. Not to mention a family dinner, with Aubrey and his sisters' significant others present, would be a good time to talk to them about the future of the ranch after Dad retired. Better still was the fact Mom, Dad and Grandma weren't going to be there.

He frowned as he recalled the conversations he'd had with Dad over the years. Victor Grandin Jr. was a good man, a strong man. He cared for his family and his children. But he wasn't what anyone would consider progressive. Like the Cattleman's Club had once been a boys' club with the archaic mantra of "No Girls Allowed," so had their father come up to believe the only person capable of running the ranch would be a son, not a daughter.

Layla was the best horse trainer Vic had ever seen, and Chelsea was dedicated to being hands-on at the ranch. She kept a close eye on their stock, which had a direct effect on the bottom line. Vic, though he could repair a fence, rope a lost calf and shoot a rogue coyote from an impressive distance, was better utilized behind the scenes. He'd been taught to view the overall workings of the ranch as one big piece, with each person in his or her sweet spot. His sisters thought he merely delegated, but there was nothing mere about running this place. It took more than a little know-how to delegate properly, which was the part they didn't see.

Regardless of what they believed he did or didn't do, his sisters' hard work and passion had been essential to the ranch. When it came to the herd or the horses, he didn't have his sisters' expertise, which was why he trusted them implicitly. It was past time he told them as much. As Aubrey had reminded him the other night, a threat to their home was the best reason for the Grandin sibs to work together.

Titan blew out a frustrated snort, stomping one foot to the ground to further voice his impatience.

"What time's dinner?" Vic asked.

Layla grinned. "Seven sharp. I hope you like Italian food."

"Everyone likes Italian food." He made a show of rolling his eyes. "I don't have to eat burgers every day, you know."

"Thanks, Vic." Her sincerity threw him a little.

"You're welcome. Hey, before you go—" He climbed on Titan's back. "Why don't you throw a saddle on one of your pet projects and come out with me? I'll race you to the east fence."

Her eyes flared with excitement. "Give me five minutes!"

She jogged to the barn as Vic broke the bad news to Titan. "We have to wait on Layla, buddy." Meanwhile, he trotted the horse in circles around the paddock to warm up. Not five minutes later, Layla came out riding a black gelding, neither of them able to contain their excitement.

"On your mark," he called out.

"Go!" Layla blazed past him.

"Shit," Vic muttered. Titan picked up on the urgency, double-timing it to catch up with Layla and her gelding.

Vic helped Aubrey out of his truck, keeping hold of her hand as they approached his family home. She expected a jolt of familiarity at the sight of the massive, elegant house. While there was a tingle of "been here before," her memories were sparse. It was almost like she hadn't been here in years. She tried to envision his bedroom but called up an image that could've been Vic's room—or a photo she saw in an issue of one of her mother's home-decorating magazines.

"Everything all right?" He stopped short of the wide front steps that led to a sprawling porch to study her in the waning light, concern etched into his forehead. He'd been checking on her a lot lately. It must be hard for him to see her like this, to worry about her recovery at a time when the family ranch should be his sole concern.

"Of course." She slapped on a smile. She wasn't going to ruin Layla's dinner tonight over nothing. When she'd bumped into Vic's sister, Aubrey had been thrilled to recognize the other woman on sight. She would have known Layla's blue eyes anywhere.

The rush of certainty had propelled her over to say hello. Layla, gracious as well as poised, had greeted Aubrey with a hug. After a short chat, Aubrey had mentioned how isolated she'd been for the last few weeks, and that's when Layla had invited her over for dinner sometime. Aubrey had accepted, and Layla promised to give Vic the details. And, apparently, the blonde middle Grandin sister had whipped together a dinner party in record time.

"What's Chelsea's fiancé's name again?" Aubrey asked as Vic opened the front door.

"Nolan Thurston, twin brother to the asshole trying to find oil on our land."

"You're not going to be like this all night, are you?" Layla was standing in the foyer, arms folded, forehead creased. "They haven't arrived yet, so you're safe."

"I don't care if they overhear," he said. Hopefully the evening went smoothly. Aubrey prickled at the idea of everyone squabbling tonight.

"So good to see you again, Aubrey. Come meet my husband, Josh." Layla led Aubrey away from Vic, who followed behind them as they stepped into the large, state-of-the-art kitchen. Josh stood at the stovetop sautéing something green. He had a muscular build, dirty-blond hair and oh—look at that—blue eyes like Layla's. They were a match made in Barbie dream heaven, an absolutely stunning couple.

Once pleasantries were exchanged and Aubrey was equipped with a glass of wine, Chelsea and Nolan let themselves in. Chelsea announced herself with a "We're here. Hold your applause!"

Nolan was tall and well-built, his features unlike Josh's in nearly every way. His hair and eyes were dark rather than light, his thick eyebrows expressive and possibly visible from space. He had a sensual smile, which was decorated with a dense five-o'clock shadow. He made a nice match for dark-haired Chelsea, whose willowy frame was draped in a fancy cocktail dress.

"What's the occasion? I've never seen you look better," Vic said, sweeping in to kiss his oldest sister's cheek.

"I know a backhanded compliment when I hear one," she returned. Before Aubrey could be properly intimidated, Chelsea turned her wide, toothy smile on her. "Aubrey Collins. How are you?"

"Good, thank you," she answered, thrown by the formality. Instinctively, she gave Chelsea a quick hug. "It's good to see you. Congratulations on your engagement."

Nolan's arm wrapped around his fiancée's waist, and Chelsea blushed prettily—a sight Aubrey had rarely, if ever, seen.

"Everyone sit! It's done!" Layla rushed by with a piping-hot dish of cheese-covered pasta. Josh followed, a platter in each hand, steam billowing in his wake.

Dinner was delicious—fettucine alfredo with slices of grilled chicken, a dish of garlicky broccolini and Texas toast slathered with butter and freshly grated Parmesan cheese.

Aubrey had eaten her fill two bites ago but couldn't help polishing off the remainder of her bread. She reclaimed her forgotten wineglass and took a sip as the vibe around the table took a turn from casual to serious.

"Since Mom and Dad are next door," Vic started, "tonight would be a good night for us to talk about the future of this ranch and what we're going to do about it."

"Which we've decided to leave to the authorities," Nolan said.

"And by *we*, I am referring to the Grandins who own this ranch, not the twin brother of the man trying to wreck it." Vic's tone was lethal.

"You're not over this yet?" Nolan tossed his napkin onto his empty plate.

"Heath trying to steal our birthrights out from under us? No, Nolan, I'm not over it."

Aubrey touched Vic's leg beneath the table. He gave her a subtle nod that said *I've got this*.

"In case you haven't noticed, Victor," Josh interjected, "we're in your sisters' lives for the long haul. Might as well accept that."

"It's Vic, and my sisters can speak for themselves. They were doing it long before either of you entered the picture." A truncated silence descended, the room buzzing with tension. Aubrey wasn't sure if the other men were being polite or if Vic's air of authority had silenced them both. Vic eased back in the formal dining chair like a cat lounging on a sundrenched windowsill. "As I was saying, the future of this ranch has always been clear. Our grandfather and our father decided when I was born that their namesake would be the one to run it."

"Oh, here we go." Chelsea held up her wineglass. "Someone top me off."

Nolan poured more red wine into her glass. Aubrey was surprised when Vic smiled.

"We know what you're going to say," Layla said. "No need to ruin everyone's evening while you restake your claim."

Vic winked at Aubrey before linking their fingers and resting their joined hands on the table. What was he up to?

"I was telling Aub about the surveyor and the problems we're having." He sent a glance to Nolan, who narrowed his gaze in response. "And she brought up a valid point. Chelsea has long believed she deserved the top spot at this ranch."

"Hello? Firstborn," Chelsea said before taking a swig from her refilled wineglass.

"You're right," Vic said.

The entire table fell silent, most notably Chelsea, who was frozen into a solid block of *Did I just hear that?* She snapped her jaw shut and shook her mane of dark brown hair. "What did you say?"

"You are a force to be reckoned with, Chels. I've always believed as much. No one works harder than you on this ranch—" he nodded at his other sister "—unless it's Layla. Believe it or not, what I do is more complicated than it looks. Logistics isn't easy with the many moving parts on this ranch. You two are amazing out there in the mix, but I was taught to run the show from a different vantage point."

"Lording over your sisters isn't a vantage point," Josh snapped.

"I wasn't lording," Vic said. "I was ensuring we turned a mean profit, a lot of which is thanks to my sisters. I could show you the financials, though I suspect my sisters have taken their fair share of peeks at them when they thought no one was looking." His pointed gaze at Chelsea and Layla drew smug smiles from both women. "I could detail the long and tiring list of blowhards I have to talk to on a routine basis to keep our prices top dollar and our reputation squeaky-clean in this industry. I suspect your talents are better utilized in your own specialties. To quote Samwise from *Lord of the Rings*, what we need to do is *share the load.* Neither of you wants to deal with the bullshit I do each day, and I don't have the skill set to do what you do."

"Did Aubrey put you up to this?" Chelsea squinted one eye in suspicion.

Aubrey didn't confirm or deny with her answer. "Sharing the responsibilities gives everyone what they want. Layla, you'll have more time with Josh on your own ranch. Chelsea, you and Nolan will have more time together as well. It will also free up Vic's time, so he can spend more of it with me." She drew their joined hands to her chest and hugged his arm. "It's win-win-win."

Vic cleared his throat, shifting slightly in his seat. Aubrey didn't mind sticking up for him. While he'd been bullheaded in the past about who should be in charge and why, he also worked very hard on this ranch.

"Thanks, Aub," came his gentle reply.

"You're welcome, Vic."

He lifted his wineglass in a toast. “From here on out, the Grandin siblings aren’t going to allow Dad to have the final say in our future. We’re going to choose our own path—the same path. There’s no sense in us veering off in three different directions when we want the same thing. Even if you two—” he nodded at Chelsea and then Layla “—take some distance from the family ranch, I will still need your input. I trust you two more than anyone. We’re stronger together.”

Layla was the first to raise her glass. “Agree. Even though you cheated when we raced to the east fence, you’re right about the ranch.”

“I didn’t cheat.” Vic’s hoisted eyebrow backed his claim. “*You* cheated. You raced that gelding out of the stable and took both Titan and me by surprise.”

“The gelding’s name is Lester. And I’m faster than you and you know it.” Layla smirked.

Chelsea raised her glass as well. “I admit, brother. I don’t want any part of what you do. Dealing with the Texas elite and their brethren requires a degree in bullshit. Which we all know you have.”

“Thank you, sis.” Vic’s sincere acceptance of the insult set off a ripple of laughter around the table. Whatever tension had snapped in the air before had been defused. Nolan and Josh and Aubrey raised their glasses, and everyone drank to the Grandin family truce.

Nine

"I'm impressed," Aubrey said as they walked outside after dinner.

Vic hadn't said what he'd said at dinner to impress her, but her approval bolstered his pride.

Night had fallen, the glow of a fat full moon cloaking the field. They passed the paddock, casting long, eerie shadows across the path where they walked.

"So, about the race to the fence. *Did* you cheat?" she asked.

"Hell no!" he answered with a laugh. "Layla raced that black beauty straight out of the stable and rode him like the hounds of hell were on her tail. Titan hates to lose almost as much as I do, though, so we nearly killed ourselves to catch up. Layla knows I won. She stopped arguing, didn't she?"

"Yeah, I guess she did. I love your sisters. They're so strong. It's enviable."

He stopped short of the stable to turn to her. "Why is it enviable? You're as strong if not stronger than either of them."

"I don't feel strong. I feel like the ghost of someone who *used* to be strong."

"Take it from me, Aub. You speak your mind, and you prioritize what matters. You don't let anyone bully you into what you don't want. Much to my chagrin, at times."

She smiled. "Because I'm not the agreeable housewife you always dreamed of?"

The comment was so close to what she'd said when they'd broken up ten years ago, his heart began galloping. If she remembered that argument, it could be the crack in the door she needed to recover the rest of her memory. He wasn't ready to let her go yet. Not when he'd just begun winning her back.

He had the acute sense he was running out of time. He knew it, even if Aubrey didn't. Her memory would surface sooner or later. He was betting on sooner, which didn't give him much time to impress upon her how much she still meant to him.

"Can I see Titan?"

"Of course."

His stallion's regal gray head was poking out of his stall when Vic and Aubrey approached. The horse blinked wide, knowing eyes when Aubrey smiled up at him.

Vic loved his horse. All horses. He was amazed by their ability to tune in to the emotions of others—

horse or human. Titan held Aubrey's gaze steadily before nudging her shoulder, his way of asking for scratches.

"The noses are the best," she murmured, stroking the baby-soft skin of the horse's muzzle. Titan closed his eyes and enjoyed Aubrey's attention. Vic knew just how Titan felt.

"He likes you."

"He probably likes everyone. Don't you, boy?"

Titan blew out a snort in response, and Aubrey laughed. Then her laugh faded as she stroked the horse's forehead. "What if I don't recover my memory?"

"You will."

"But what if I *don't*?" Her green eyes were filled with fear and curiosity in equal measures. She was asking him for honesty, something he'd been half-assing since he agreed to step back into her life. So, he told her the truth.

"If you don't, you don't." He shrugged. "Your doc won't keep you from work forever. And after you're cleared, you won't have to live with your parents like I do."

"In such squalor." She gestured in the direction of the house.

It was good to see her smile. He wished she'd keep smiling. He could only imagine how frustrating it was not to be able to fill in the gaps of her memory. Which was partially why he tipped his head and asked, "Want to see the loft?"

She screwed her lips to one side. "Should I be suspicious of your motives?"

"No. Well. Maybe." He claimed her hand and led her away. Titan complained about the loss of attention, but Vic mentally promised to give the horse extra scratches for his gentlemanly behavior. He released Aubrey's hand and nodded to the set of stairs leading to the top of the stable. They were new, unstained and smelled of fresh pine.

"These weren't always here," she said. "There was a ladder, right?"

"See? Your memory's returning already. Go on. I'll follow you up." He grabbed a clean blanket from the stack on the shelf, figuring the horses wouldn't mind if he borrowed one.

She walked up the stairs, and he followed close behind in case she lost her balance. He was playing with fire bringing her up here, but she would only have good memories of him if she had any at all. He certainly hadn't forgotten the nights they'd spent up here after dark, the moonlight slatting through the open window while they lay naked on a bed of fresh straw.

"Haven't done this in a while," he confessed as she wandered around the spacious loft. He hadn't ever brought another woman here, and he hadn't brought Aubrey since they were young. It was sacred, this space. And like he'd time traveled back to those days, he had the sudden urge to take off her clothes. To make love to her while confessing how she still tied him up in knots.

"What's wrong?" she asked, picking up on his silence.

Too many things to mention. He shook his head and confessed, “Maybe this is a bad idea.”

Fingertips stroking a hay bale, she turned to face him. His anguished expression said what he wouldn’t.

He was worried about her. He’d shadowed her every footfall as she’d climbed the stairs, his arms open to catch her. Her knight in a black Stetson. He hadn’t worn the hat tonight, which gave her an unobstructed view of the concern etched across his forehead. Moonlight caught the angles of his hard jaw as well as the feisty bad-boy glint in his eyes that’d been there before he’d reconsidered his intentions.

She took the blanket from his hands. “I know what you’re worried about.”

“You do?” His Adam’s apple bobbed as he folded his arms over his chest.

“Yes.” She wasn’t going to let him ruin this evening, not when they both wanted the same thing. She untucked her plaid shirt from her jeans. “You’re trying to take it easy on me because I’m injured. You’re worried that you’ll cause a setback for me, and then you’ll never forgive yourself for it.” She unbuttoned the bottom two buttons of her shirt. He watched as she slipped each pearlescent button through the fabric. “You have to trust that I know what’s best for me.”

She finished unbuttoning the shirt, noting the exact moment the worry left Vic’s expression and dark hunger overtook it. She tossed the shirt aside.

He took another step closer to her, his hands going to her waist.

The only sounds around them were the occasional whinny from downstairs and the tight, anticipatory breaths she was taking. She turned her attention to the buttons on his shirt next. “I remember.”

His voice was a dry husk when he asked, “What do you remember?”

“Stargazing on horseback.” She plucked at another button. “Whispering as we checked the stable to see if your daddy or any ranch hands were in here. Climbing up into this loft with a blanket and a stolen bottle of whiskey from your parents’ liquor cabinet.”

He grinned. “Our getaway.”

“As if your enormous family home hadn’t offered enough privacy.”

“You liked it outside better,” he said.

“I liked it with you any way I could get it, Vic Grandin.” She opened his unbuttoned shirt and smoothed her hands over his heated skin. Firm pecs, the perfect sprinkle of chest hair and a taut belly. He was a beautiful specimen of a man. And he was all man. Not the skinnier version of the boy she’d fallen in love with, though he was there, too. She could see the nervous twitch of that boy’s smile. She placed a kiss on his chest, closing her lips over his bare skin as she inhaled. His cedar-and-citrus scent mingled with the fragrance of hay, taking her back in time ten years.

He tipped her chin as she was about to kiss his chest again. “Aubrey, before you—”

“I trust you. More than anyone. Now you have to

trust me. You're right. I'm strong. I know what I can handle and what I can't." She pulled his belt free, snaking the thick leather through his belt loops and tossing it to the floor. "I can handle you."

"That a fact?" His smile returned, the lust in his eyes crowding out his earlier concern.

"Why don't you try me and find out, cowboy?" She cupped where his jeans tented, finding him primed and hard for her. He held himself in check, but only barely. His nostrils flared. His gaze rerouted to the overflowing cups of her bra.

He tugged her close, dipping his face until his lips hovered a hairsbreadth above hers. "Last chance."

She pushed to her toes and crushed her lips to his, hugging his neck and pressing her breasts against his chest. He bent and lifted her, cradling her ass in his wide hands as she wrapped her legs around his body. Then he moved to a hay bale and plopped her onto it, where they made out long and slow.

His mouth slanted over hers, hungry and impatient, the pace intentional. Every part of her body responded, from her tightening nipples to the liquid heat pooling in her belly. She wiggled and squirmed as he stroked her tongue with his, seeking relief where she needed it most.

He'd always been good at this. She had been kissing Vic for years and had never once been disappointed. He poured his entire self into a kiss. Everything he wanted to say but didn't. Whenever they were physically together, nothing else mattered. Not time or place or any argument they'd had about their combined futures.

Eyes shut, she pulled her lips from his. That thought tried to unlock the door to another, but the key wouldn't quite turn.

Vic kissed the side of her throat once, twice, while she waited for clarity to come. It vanished before a memory could form. When his lips hit the tender skin behind her ear, she stopped her mental struggle. Time was the key to her healing. Time, and really delicious sex with her boyfriend.

She unbuttoned his jeans and unzipped his fly, wedging her hand behind the stiff denim. What she encountered was smooth, thick and long, and guaranteed to make her smile. The last time they'd slept together had been the night before her accident, which was way too long ago for her taste.

Vic, no longer arguing about her health, kicked off his boots and shucked his clothes. He helped her off the bale and out of her clothes next, resting his lips over hers as he laid her out on the blanket.

He worked his way down her throat, then glided his tongue along her collarbone. By the time he set his mouth to her nipple, he'd reduced her to a pleading, panting woman with only one thing on her mind.

"Please, what?" He smiled against her breast, his inhalation leaving goose bumps on her skin.

"Don't tease me," she warned, but she barely meant it. She couldn't remember feeling this carefree before. Had she?

"Yes, ma'am." He kissed his way down her stomach and to her hip bones before settling between her legs. Once there, he knew how to please her—slow, then fast, before slowing down again. She clutched his hair in one fist, arched her neck and gave in. He was in control of her pleasure, leaving her free to float untethered, no worries clogging her mind.

Moments later, she gave in to pleasure so acute she almost couldn't bear it. She muffled her cries with one hand until Vic surfaced and replaced that hand with his mouth. And while she was kissing him, she felt a single tear leak from each eye that she didn't bother hiding.

Ten

On the night they'd spent together after he'd sworn they'd never sleep together again, caution had closely followed their orgasms. Now there were no roped-off areas, no caution lingering in her eyes, no awkward covering of her naked body. She was the picture of bliss. Her eyes were drawn, her smile adorably goofy, and she was laid out nude like she was as unashamed as she'd ever been with him.

It was hell leaving her to dispose of the condom, but he did, taking care to tug on his jeans before jogging down the stairs. He returned to the loft to find her sitting on the center of the blanket, wearing naught but his plaid shirt.

He'd thought he preferred her naked to clothed,

until she was covered in his navy-and-green flannel. *Because she belongs with you.*

Guilt spiked in the center of his chest, but he told it to go to hell. She'd assured him that she trusted him. She'd reminded him that she knew what she wanted. He couldn't regret what had just happened if he tried.

Nothing had felt more right than sliding into her, watching her eyes sink shut and her mouth drop open. Unless it was the moment she'd wrapped her legs around his back and scratched her fingernails across his shoulders. That'd felt pretty damn right, too.

"I thought I was too full for that sort of acrobatic workout." She emitted a throaty laugh. "Guess not."

He crossed to where she sat and folded her against him, moving the collar of the shirt to the side to place a kiss on her neck. "Were you cold?"

"I was, but with you here I'm not. If we were in your room or my apartment, I'd still be naked. Is that incentive enough for you to take me indoors?"

As if he needed more incentive than her cries coating his ear canal as she came. Although, his bedroom held memories that could thwart his plan to win her back. He frowned, considering. She'd seen the ranch, been inside the house, chatted with his sisters. And then there was the loft. Aubrey hadn't had a memory that would endanger this version of them...*yet.*

She leaned back against his chest and let out a sigh. He knew her sounds—even after not being with her for years, he still knew them.

"Something on your mind other than round two?" He hugged her waist, and she held his hands, toying with his fingers in silence before she finally answered him.

"Are you planning on getting married?"

His nose in her hair, he inhaled, unsure how to respond.

"We've had to have talked about it. Humor me, and remind me why we've been dating since the age of sixteen and haven't progressed past sex in the loft." She twisted her neck to look over her shoulder at him. "That wasn't a complaint, by the way."

He could lie and say they'd been too busy to talk about it, or he could tell her the truth, which was that they'd been engaged once, but she'd changed her mind. Vic had promised to do what was best for her in this situation, and in no way was reminding her of a tumultuous time ten years ago helpful to her recovery. When he answered, he let his reply hover in between truth and fiction.

"We've talked about marriage. Like moving in together, the timing wasn't right for us." He didn't think he'd ever spoken truer words about his and Aubrey's relationship.

After they'd broken up, he'd been angry. He couldn't fathom why she'd throw away everything they'd built. He'd known in his gut she'd never find someone better than him. When he'd returned to the world of dating, he'd had a similar epiphany—he'd never found anyone like Aubrey.

The women he'd dated had been beautiful, intelligent, self-starters. Sleeping with them had rewarded him with physical relief, but he'd never found the connection he'd had with Aubrey. Over the years, it'd become painfully clear he'd never find the solace he'd found in her. Aubrey was his own personal Halley's Comet. Once in a lifetime, and he'd never believed he'd be lucky enough to have her come around again.

When he'd propositioned her at the Silver Saddle, the ache in his chest had been unbearable. The morning after their incredible night together, he'd walked away, reminding himself of his promise to her. He'd told her it'd be like the sex had never happened. He'd meant it at the time. Having her back in his life and knowing there'd be no happy ending for them would be sheer torture.

Now he was in some sort of bizarre limbo. She hadn't forgotten the night they spent together, but her mind had altered the circumstances surrounding it. She didn't remember their agreement. She'd woven their steamy night between the sheets with the people they'd been prebreakup. Back when she'd been his world, and he'd been hers.

Until she'd gone to college.

He used to tell himself she'd changed when she went to school, but now he understood that she'd become more of who she already was. She cared about others, revered education and was warm and patient with everyone she encountered. He'd admired her abilities and her intelligence, but he'd also been blind.

He'd been solely focused on himself—on his legacy. His father was the king, the ranch his castle. Victor Jr. saw Vic as the prince who'd be crowned after he retired. Vic had been raised to believe that he knew better than anyone—his mother and grandmother, his sisters and Aubrey included—what was best for the Grandin family. He'd never stopped to question if that was true or not.

To him, Aubrey's interest in graduate school hadn't been about her pursuing her dreams, it'd been about delaying each rite of passage on the way to his ultimate goal: inheriting the ranch. When she'd told him she wasn't ready to be a mother, he'd had a vision of his future kingdom crumbling. He didn't have a backup plan. His father hadn't asked his opinion about the ranch or his future but had simply told Vic what was expected of him. And Vic, in his attempt to appease his father and step up and be the man he'd been tasked with becoming, had argued with Aubrey and had ultimately lost her.

He'd failed at strong-arming her into doing what he wanted. Was it any wonder she'd decided not to marry him? Had their roles been reversed, he never would have stayed with her. He wouldn't have changed his lifelong goals for anyone.

He'd been so shortsighted.

Thankfully, Vic wasn't a cocky twenty-one-year-old anymore. He was a grown man navigating the choppy waters of real life. With the threat of losing the ranch his family treasured, and possibly losing Aubrey for a second time.

She impatiently tapped her fingers on his hand before unhooking his arms from her waist and moving away from him. She stood and pulled on her jeans, her movements jerky.

“Where are you going?”

“Just say it, Vic. You’re not interested in marrying me. I don’t need my memory back to know that. Your stony silence says everything you’re not.” She pulled off his shirt and tossed it at his face, redressing quickly, her back to him. “I don’t believe you’re being careful because of my injury. You’re like this all the time, aren’t you?”

“Like what?”

“Distant.”

He bit his tongue to keep from explaining how she had no idea how *distant* he’d been during their decade-long separation. Though that might have been a better option than what he said next. “I’ve always wanted to marry you, Aubrey.”

Her green eyes widened. He stood and yanked on his shirt. “Come on.”

She eyed his outstretched hand nervously.

“I’m not going to let you stand here and say things that aren’t true. You said you could handle me, right?”

She blinked at his palm one final time before sliding her hand into his. He led her from the loft, along the gravel path and up the stairs to his private entrance.

She’d said he didn’t want to marry her, but nothing could have been further from the truth. Hell, if he’d known then what he knew now, he would’ve fought harder for them, and damn his stupid pride.

Vic opened the private entryway to his suite, ushering Aubrey through the doorway ahead of him. She navigated a short hallway that opened to a small kitchenette on the left. His bedroom was on the right, if it could even be called that. The massive space held a wide bed with rich mahogany-colored leather head- and footboards. A matching leather sofa and recliner faced a large-screen TV, and in the corner of the room was a desk and a tall shelf lined with books. It was like his own apartment nestled inside the house. A corridor past the kitchen opened to a sizable bathroom with one other doorway bisecting that hallway.

When she faced Vic, she found him watching her carefully. He was standing at his dresser, top drawer pulled open. He motioned for her to come to him, and she did, each footfall leaden with inexplicable dread.

No memories came, only a strange, disembodied sensation. He plucked a pale gray velvet box from the drawer and then opened it to reveal a platinum wedding band set. A chunky diamond surrounded by other smaller diamonds winked in the bedroom's ambient light, and her breath grew stale in her lungs.

"I've had this ring in my drawer for ten years. We disagreed about the future—you wanted a different life than I wanted. It's not that I didn't want to marry you, Aub. Like I told you, the timing was wrong."

The ring was beautiful. She didn't know much about jewelry. She didn't know the name of this particular shape of diamond. She didn't need to know anything except what it represented: a future—their future. One that Vic had planned for with her in mind. Standing here, the ring in its box mere inches away, she suddenly wanted the future it promised more than anything.

With a shaking hand, she plucked the ring from its velvet bed. "I can't believe it."

"I don't know how else to prove it to you."

She peered up at him, the diamond band between them. "You've had this for ten years?"

He nodded. "Every last one of them."

"You didn't give up."

"No. I guess I didn't." He gently took the ring from her grasp and tucked it back into the box, shutting the lid. It was like watching her future recede into the distance. She'd already lost a chunk of her past. Losing her future as well was unacceptable.

"You wanted to marry me, but you never asked."

He placed the box back in the dresser drawer but said nothing.

"And now? Are you waiting until I regain my memory? Are you worried if I don't, you won't be interested in spending a lifetime with me?" She could almost understand that way of thinking. What if she backslid? Or had health problems that affected her for years to come? How could she expect him to stay by her side and care for her when he could live an unburdened life without her?

"No." He gripped her upper arms and bent to look into her eyes. "Listen to me carefully, Aubrey Leann Collins. Me wanting to marry you has nothing to do with your memory or lack thereof. But…"

"But?"

"*You* wanting to marry *me* has everything to do with it."

She shook her head, the riddle making no sense to her. He spoke before she could argue.

"Trust me, beautiful. If I thought it was fair to you, I'd move heaven and earth to marry you as soon as possible. You deserve a big proposal and a bigger wedding. You also deserve to know—to remember—the facts before you agree to spend a lifetime with me."

"Why wouldn't I want to marry you?" She wrapped her arms around his neck and met his honest, espresso-brown eyes. "I love you. I've always loved you."

He looked lost for a moment, his eyebrows bent, his mouth pulling down at the corners.

"Vic. I love—"

He smothered the sentiment with a kiss. A long, lovely kiss she found it so easy to lose herself in. His arms embraced her, hugging her close as he drank her in for a leisurely minute. When his lips left hers, she hummed in her throat.

"Fair warning," she whispered. "When you ask, I'll say yes. We'll move into our own home and have a few Grandin babies. A whole new generation will inherit your family's ranch. How's that sound?"

His expression of disbelief faded into one hot enough to burn down the entire house. She'd settle for igniting the sheets.

"Let's try out your bed."

"Good idea," he growled and then, once again, stripped off her clothes.

Eleven

Aubrey twisted her hands as Dr. Mitchell thumbed through a stack of papers. She'd spent most of a day last week at the doctor's office, undergoing a battery of tests to determine if there'd been any improvement. The other woman hummed, then nodded, then hummed again.

"I'm pleasantly surprised." Dr. Mitchell's kind smile made the good news better.

Aubrey let out a nervous laugh, notably relieved. "I was worried you'd tell me something I didn't want to hear."

"I might. But overall, I'm pleased with your progress."

Aubrey wasn't. Over the last month, she'd been the opposite of barraged with memories of her life.

The recollections came more as a trickle, and even then they weren't complete. Though she'd recalled many bits and pieces of her life, a significant chunk of her memory was AWOL.

"You have had many memories, and better yet, you haven't forgotten anything from the last few days." Dr. Mitchell set the paperwork aside. "According to Vic, anyway. You two have been spending a lot of time together."

"Yes." She'd filled out the questionnaire and then had asked him to corroborate her memories. As the doctor had mentioned when Aubrey had picked up the forms, "There's no other way for me to know if the new memories you're creating are sticking."

Aubrey had joked to Vic about leaving out her *stickiest* memories of the loft and the time spent in his bedroom. He had given her a wicked grin and said, "I'll spare your doctor the filthy, fantastic facts, but you should feel free to share them with me in as much detail as possible. And if you'd like a reenactment, just yell."

She'd been understandably nervous about the assessment. Would Dr. Mitchell tell Aubrey that she was healing too slowly? Would any of her answers trigger a warning?

"Does this mean I can return to work?" Aubrey asked.

"You're close, but not yet. I'd like to see a bit more progress before you take on the stressors of returning to the workforce."

"But I—"

"You love your job. I understand, Ms. Collins,

but good stress is still stress. I would also prefer you didn't drive yet, as an extra precaution."

Aubrey let out a frustrated sigh and then blurted, "What about riding a horse?" She'd wanted to climb onto Titan the moment she'd laid eyes on him.

"This is a common question among you Texans," Dr. Mitchell said with a chuckle. She stacked the paperwork and tucked it into the file by her elbow. "I moved here from Chicago, and after nearly eight years, I still can't wrap my head around those animals."

Just when Aubrey thought her request would be denied, the doctor continued, "No *bronco* riding, but if you want to go for a steady trot, I don't see the harm. Navigating an open pasture is different from changing lanes in thick freeway traffic. Give me the benefit of not worrying about you behind the wheel yet. Okay?"

"Okay." Aubrey would take the win. A tepid trot on horseback was at least some forward progress. She exited the doctor's office and found her mother in the waiting room. Aubrey quickly relayed the state of her health as they walked out of the hospital and to her mother's car.

"Will you drop me off at the Grandin ranch? I want to surprise Vic."

"I don't care what your doctor says, I'm not comfortable with you riding a horse." Mary's mouth pulled into a frown as she steered out of the parking lot.

"It's not like I'm in a rodeo. I miss riding. I feel like it's been forever."

"Ever since you and Vic—" Her mother shook her head as she drove.

"Ever since me and Vic what?"

"You stopped riding ten years ago."

Funny how that timeline seemed to coincide with not only her memories of him, but also the engagement ring hiding in his drawer. "Why?"

"You were focused on college."

Again with the college excuse? Hadn't she known that it was possible to be, do and have more than life as a college student? She understood pursuing her beloved profession had taken dedicated attention, but what about the years after she'd earned her degree? Why hadn't she returned to doing what she'd loved before? Like riding horses, or marrying her freaking boyfriend?

"I'm not allowed to go back to work yet, so this is the first good news I've had in a while. I'd appreciate if you didn't ruin it for me," Aubrey clipped. Her frustration was aimed at the wrong person, but she couldn't help herself. "I will call a car service from your house if you refuse to take me to see him."

"All right, all right. Goodness, you're spirited today." Mary sounded reluctant when she admitted, "I've missed this side of you. Maybe this incident is a blessing in disguise."

Aubrey liked the sound of that, especially since she had been enjoying her life lately. She had no way of knowing if she was behaving differently than normal—but she had zero complaints.

As her mother pulled into the Grandin ranch and parked next to the stable, she warned Aubrey for the fifteenth time to be safe. Aubrey promised she would and then practically ran from the car in pursuit of her newfound freedom.

An absolutely gorgeous redhead was angling for the front door of the ranch house, wearing a sexy floral dress and a pair of cowboy boots. Vic barely suppressed a smile as he cupped his palms around his mouth and shouted Aubrey's name.

She turned and started his way, her soft auburn waves lifting on the breeze. He loved when she wore her hair down. And when she flashed him a dazzling grin, he felt Cupid's arrow slide into his chest for the felling blow.

It was official. Vic was a goner for Aubrey Collins once again.

She broke into a run toward him, which caused another arrhythmic pattern in his heart. He caught her, hugging her close and inhaling the clean sunshine scent of her hair.

"The doctor cleared me to ride," she said as he set her feet back onto the ground. "Let's throw a saddle on Titan and take him out!"

Her eyes twinkled as she turned her head to look toward the stable where he'd just been. When she looked back at him and took in the state of his dust-covered attire, she frowned. "You're a mess."

"Thanks." He swiped hay off his sleeves. "I was helping the stable hands feed the horses. I've been enjoying being out here in the elements lately. A good leader should know what the hell's going on with his ranch."

She propped her hand on her hip. "And this has nothing to do with proving to your sisters that you're more than a delegator?"

"That's…secondary." He palmed the back of his neck, uncharacteristically sheepish. "Are you sure you want to take Titan out now?"

"Yes! I'm like a jack-in-the-box that's been wound too tight. I have so much pent-up energy I feel like I'm going to explode. I want you to ride with me. Keep me safe."

He found it particularly hard to say no to her when she appealed to his protective side. If he was sure of one capability in his arsenal, it was that he could keep Aubrey safe—especially from the vantage point of atop a horse.

"I have a confession first," she said.

His heart sputtered to a halt as his mind introduced any number of memories she might confess. Had she remembered one of their arguments? *The* argument? "Oh yeah?"

"I don't remember Titan, and I don't know why."

Well, *he* knew why she didn't know Titan. Aubrey had been long gone from Vic's life when he'd bought the horse five years ago. With no easy way to explain that, he said, "Titan responds to the genuineness of a person. And you, Aubrey," he said, taking her hand and leading her to the stable, "are as genuine as they come."

He made short work of saddling up the horse. Titan was a gentle giant and had never been interested in tossing anyone off his back. Seeing Aubrey topple off that stage the night of the pool party had shaved years off Vic's life. If the unthinkable happened and she fell off his horse, he'd throw himself off with her if he had a shot at preventing her from injury.

He helped her into the saddle and then joined her. Titan seemed to intuitively know he was carrying precious cargo. The horse took them the easy way, his gait rhythmic as he followed the fence line. It felt right to have Aubrey's hair tickling Vic's cheeks, her back leaning against his front as they rode.

They used to ride together, around the ranch. She always wanted to pet the cows, and he'd gotten the biggest kick out of that. Back then, while he'd respected and cared for the animals, he'd looked at them more like a commodity than living beings. Aubrey had opened his eyes to the kindness in theirs, to the literal sacrifice they were making so that Vic and his family could live a good life. He'd gained a lot of respect for the living, breathing creatures that were a part of this ranch. Aubrey had changed him for the better in that way—and countless others.

The midday sun played in her hair, which glimmered like spun, copper-colored silk. Having her around this last month was the ultimate second chance. Like in the movie *It's a Wonderful Life*, Vic was destined to wake out of the alternate reality to find everything as it had been. And when she remembered everything and resented him for playing her, he'd already decided what to do.

He was going to fight for her until his dying breath.

He hadn't fought for her when she left the first time. That was a mistake he refused to repeat.

"I remember this," she gasped. She snapped her head around to look up at him. "Vic, I *remember* riding with you. I'm sorry I stopped. I was so focused on school."

He didn't correct her, though he knew the real reason why she'd quit riding. It was because she'd never come to see him after the breakup. That night had been so final, so ruinous, they hadn't even managed to salvage a friendship.

"God. It's like it happened yesterday," she continued. "Isn't time weird?"

"The weirdest." He'd been having major flashbacks himself.

"I just… I wish I could remember more. Dr. Mitchell told me not to worry, but how am I supposed to do that?"

"You never liked being out of control."

"You're one to talk."

"We had that in common. Which is probably why…" *We argued so much about our future.* "Why, uh, we've butted heads on occasion."

"How else could we be so skilled at the making-up part?" She rested her head against his shoulder. When he thought of the years they could have spent fighting and making up, his heart crushed like an empty soda can.

"If you want to pick a fight with me, Aubrey Collins, knock yourself out. Not literally, though." He tightened his hold on her, and she freed an elbow and shot it into his ribs.

"That was bad."

"How bad?"

"*Bad* bad."

This was the Aubrey he remembered. Paired with a kinder, tenderer version of himself that he remembered. He hadn't always been a stubborn ass who wanted to corral her. In the beginning, he'd liked the way she challenged him. Once the power she'd managed to wield effortlessly had overtaken him, though, he'd been scared down to his spurs.

His grandfather and father ran the literal roost, and Vic had mistakenly believed, as the only Grandin son, that would also be his job. He'd been inexperienced both in relationships and in managing a ranch this size. He'd feared that taking an ounce of attention off his work would cause the entire outfit to collapse.

When Aubrey had insisted on continuing on to graduate school, he'd seen no pros, only cons. The idea of her stressed about earning a decent salary, or her fate being chosen by faceless city board members, drove him crazy. It was Vic's job to take care of her. She was his princess, and he'd wanted to build a carefree life for her. And he could admit to the sliver of doubt that'd crept in when her drive and ambition had made it seem like he hadn't offered her enough.

He'd been immature and shortsighted, and they'd lost years together because of it. Well, this time he wouldn't go down without a fight. She belonged with him.

She always had.

Twelve

"What is that?" A reddish-brown lump in the golden brush stirred and then stilled just as quickly. The small, round, fur-covered animal was breathing. She could see its back lifting and dropping.

"A calf slipped through the fence. He's hiding," Vic answered.

A mournful wail came from the calf's mother, a brown-and-white cow, mooing her warning to Vic—or maybe encouragement to her little one. The calf didn't move a muscle.

"Is he hurt?" she asked as Titan's head came up, the muscles on his flanks tightening beneath her legs.

Vic leaned forward and whispered one word. "Coyote."

Her eyes followed his pointing finger to the thin

dog lurking beyond the brush. If it cared that they were there, it didn't show. Its predatory gaze was locked on the calf.

"Where there's one, there's more," Vic murmured.

"That's not very reassuring."

"No. It's not."

He dismounted, skirted the calf's hiding place and began whistling and clapping at the coyote and its unseen pack. Only then she did see them—and hear them—as they yipped and ran off into the trees beyond the field.

The mother cow mooed her concern. Vic reassured her with, "I'll get your baby. Don't worry."

From his belt, he unclipped a rope and fashioned a lasso. His second toss landed around the calf's neck. Only then did the calf burst to life, struggling to escape while its mother wailed in protest. Aubrey's heart lurched. She had a soft spot for animals, and clearly neither of them understood that Vic was trying to help.

Thankfully, he returned the calf to the safety of the other side of the fence mere moments later. Once the baby was reunited with its mother, the larger cow licked and doted.

Aubrey smiled at the sweet interaction. "She's a good mama."

"She is." He watched the scene for a moment before he looked up at her, eyes squinting against the sun in spite of the Stetson on his head. "You were the one who taught me that, you know. You were always pointing out the beauty in these beasts. I never noticed before I met you."

He climbed back into Titan's saddle and wrapped his arms around her waist. Together they watched as the lost duo rejoined the herd on the hill.

Once they were out of sight, she rested her hand on his and said, "You'll make a good daddy."

The rigid set of his arms around her communicated that the compliment might have fallen short. Had the topic of children been hallowed ground? Something they'd spoken of in the past or, possibly, *argued* about? She had a funny feeling they had alternate viewpoints on the topic.

"I always thought so."

She didn't miss the note of wonder in his voice. "And I didn't?"

He guided Titan back to the trail. "It was less about me, more about you."

She was a teacher. She loved children. It would make sense if she'd been eager to have a family of her own. Had she postponed one love for the other? The more she learned about her past, the less she wanted to remember.

They rode silently for a few minutes before she spoke again. "Thanks for bringing me out. If you're too busy to give me a ride home, I can call a car."

He surprised her by saying, "Or you can stay with me."

"Really?"

"Yes, really," he answered with a soft chuckle. "Call your parents and let them know I'll bring you by in the morning. In the meantime, I have a shower with our names on it."

She warmed at the idea that she hadn't spoiled the

mood tonight by reminding him how difficult she'd been about their future. "A shower sounds lovely."

"Wait'll you see what I do to you in that shower," he said against her ear. "I'm going to make sure you never forget how good you had it with me."

"What do you mean, *had*?" She twisted her neck to look up at him. "Are you going somewhere?"

"Not by choice, Aubrey with the auburn hair. Not by choice."

Titan trotted, steady and slow, as Vic guided him up onto a small hill. The sun was dipping low in the sky, the trees along the horizon black silhouettes. She sat, Vic's arms wrapped around her waist, his cheek against hers, while they watched until the last dab of light slipped behind the mountains.

So, her life hadn't been perfect. And there were parts she couldn't remember, for reasons she couldn't comprehend. What had happened in the past no longer mattered, not when everything felt so right in the moment.

When she was with Vic, she knew all she needed to know. She knew she loved him and he loved her—the fact he hadn't said it yet hadn't escaped her attention, and there was an engagement ring in his dresser drawer meant for her. She'd been trying not to think too hard about what he said about her changing her mind after her memory returned. Everything about him screamed that he was a man who'd never abandon or betray her. What more was there to know?

She reached behind her and wrapped one arm around his neck. He kissed her cheek as the breeze blew, bringing with it the sweet smells of wildflowers and grass.

She had tied herself to this man fourteen years ago. She trusted her decisions. She knew what was best for her.

"Vic?"

"Yeah, honey."

"About that shower…"

His low chuckle vibrated along her back. "You got it," he said before clucking his tongue at Titan. They silently trotted back to the stable.

With Aubrey in the privacy of his suite, Vic kicked off his boots and reached for the stud on his jeans. Aubrey, a playful glint in her eyes, lifted the skirt of her floral dress to show her thighs, and then her panties, before dropping it to hide them from view. She repeated the dance while he wrestled with his jeans, too engrossed by the show to pay a damn bit of attention to what he was doing.

When she whipped the dress off and threw it at his chest, he nearly tripped over the stray leg of his jeans on his way to her. He caught her at the dresser, backing her against it to give her a thorough kiss.

Then his mind strayed to the box in the top drawer.

To the very engagement ring Aubrey had returned to him with no intention of taking it back. The same Aubrey who had just assured him he'd make a good father, and who continually asked about their future. A future that, until very recently, had been a pipe dream.

"Are you okay?" she breathed. Her lips were swollen from his kisses, her chest flushed pink and her nipples pressing the thin fabric of her bra.

"Yeah." He dived back into the sanctuary of her mouth, unbuttoning his shirt and tossing it behind him. "We have to take a shower first." He gave her one more fast kiss. "I smell like cow."

"You smell like *you*." Her eyes flashed, an undeniable heat communicating how much she wanted him. That look poured itself into the center of his chest, where a groove of longing had been carved over the long and lonely decade he'd spent missing her.

She pulled down the cups of her pale yellow lace bra to flash him. Just as quickly, she covered herself, her hands going to her matching panties next. Her panties had *always* matched her bras. God, he loved this woman.

The thought stopped him cold. Of course he knew that—he'd known that. He'd refrained from telling her because it wouldn't be fair to her. When she remembered everything, he needed her to understand he hadn't been simply toying with her heart this second time around. He was here for the long haul—if she'd have him.

Big if.

"Don't you like yellow?" She arched her back, and he closed his larger hands over the most exquisite breasts he'd ever seen, felt or tasted.

"Hate it," he lied. "I'd better take this off." He unhooked her bra, and it followed the same path to the floor his shirt had. Her breasts were a perfect handful. The first time he'd seen those pale peach nipples, he'd been a slack-jawed seventeen-year-old with the most painful erection of his life to date. He felt a similar way seeing them now. Even after he'd had them on his tongue countless times. Even after he'd plucked them to eager peaks while making love to her the other night.

He rolled his boxer briefs off his legs, his erection springing free. Aubrey lost the panties, throwing them at his face. He caught them midair, his reflexes every bit what they used to be, and chased her across the bedroom to the shower. She didn't resist him long. He pressed every naked inch of her against every naked inch of him as he blindly felt for the shower door. He tested the water, determined it was the ideal temperature and shoved them both inside.

"I miss this." She sighed against his lips as rivulets of water rolled off her chin.

"Me, too." He blinked, the shower spray bouncing off his cheeks. He didn't know if she meant that she'd remembered the times they'd showered together or if she was being hyperbolic, but he sure as hell meant it. He missed this. He missed *her*. He missed every second of holding her close and kissing her. Of seeing her matching panties and bras. He'd lost years thanks to his own stubbornness. He refused to rush tonight.

Lowering his face, he kissed her slower this time, pushing his tongue past her lips to savor her heady flavor. When she moaned into his mouth, he coasted one palm along her ribs and cupped one of her breasts in his hand. He took one succulent peach nipple between his thumb and forefinger, then flattened her back against the tile wall.

His eyes drilling into hers, he ran his other hand down her torso until he reached her center. She widened her stance in silent permission, giving him ample room to play. The trust between them was a major turn-on. Her auburn curls tickled his fingers and then he slid home, pushing into her wetness with two fingers as his thumb played her clit.

"You're smoking hot, Aubrey Collins." He nibbled her bottom lip, watching as her green irises were swallowed by black pupils. "Do you like this?"

"Yes." She shuddered as steam rose around them.

"No one can turn you on the way I do. No one can make you feel as good as I make you feel." He had the urgent need to claim her. To remind her, so that when she did remember, she would search as fruitlessly as he had for a replacement, and, like him, she would fail to find one. He didn't doubt that she'd experienced someone else in their time apart, but he wanted her to know she wouldn't have to stoop ever again. He'd be here—he'd always be here.

"Yes." Her eyes rolled back into her head as he continued touching her and turning her on. She'd only be satisfied by him from here on out.

"Say it."

"Just you, Vic. Only you."

He hadn't fully earned this woman, but pride laced through him all the same. He ended the kiss when her breathing increased, her tiny mewls prefacing her inevitable climax. Because he could take her there. No one else.

Not ever again.

"There, *there.*" She gripped his wrist, and he zeroed in on her clitoris. Stroking her diligently, he kept his gaze locked onto her beautiful face while he worked. There was nothing better in this life than watching her come. From the heated flush that worked its way from her chest to her cheeks, to the way she squeezed her eyes closed, to the moan escaping her lush mouth.

Awestruck, he witnessed all three, wrapping his free arm around her to keep her from sliding down the shower wall.

He wanted nothing but to line up to her entrance and slide home. To feel her clutch around him and hear her breathy pants in his ear. To pound them into a merciful oblivion until they were so weak from the effort, they'd be forced to sleep on a pile of towels on the bathroom floor.

Her eyes opened lazily, a wonky smile following.

"We need a condom," he huffed, the words ragged. He dropped his forehead to hers in defeat.

"But I like it in here." She pushed her bottom lip out into a pout.

"You'll like it out there, too, where I can maneuver." He cupped each side of her face and kissed her, then made the epically difficult decision to stop. "What was I saying?"

"You were talking about maneuvering." She spun off the shower knob. "I can't wait to see what comes next."

"*You* come next." He dragged her from the shower, leaving a river of water from their dripping bodies as he angled for the bed. "Then it's my turn."

Thirteen

"These sheets are soaked," Aubrey complained as she sat up, her bare back chilly and damp.

"You're welcome." Vic was lying on top of his bedding next to her, wearing nothing but a smug and wholly sexy smirk. Her eyes lingered on the valleys and grooves of his abs and pectoral muscles. The broad shoulders. The penis that was no less impressive at half-mast and resting on one thigh. She'd always loved the shape of him. Even the hair under his arms and on his chest and legs turned her on.

"Soaked from the shower water." She threw a pillow at him.

He pulled the pillow away from his stupidly handsome face to reveal he was grinning, too. How could either of them do anything short of grinning like fools after what they'd done? First off, it was fun. Secondly, it was *damn fun.*

"What were we thinking, not drying off first?"

He looped an arm around her waist and tugged. She yelped as she landed ungracefully on top of him. Once there, she decided to stay, her nude body stuck to his. This was easily the most confusing time of her life, and yet she had no problem finding an immense amount of joy.

"We've perfected sex," she told him.

His grin broadened. "You think so?"

"I think so. Don't you?"

"I *know* so. Everyone else in the world believes they're having amazing sex. They have no idea we're the ones having the best sex possible."

She kissed him lightly. "Poor souls."

"I won't tell if you don't," he whispered against her mouth. Something about his smile reminded her of the tender way they'd fallen for each other when they were teenagers. Vic Grandin was, like his name, *grand.* He'd walked around their high school like he'd owned the place. And when her mother overheard her saying so, Mary Collins had concluded, "He probably does. Do you know who his father is?"

Aubrey had been accepted by the Grandins from the moment Vic introduced her to his family. Layla and Chelsea and even protective, younger Morgan had liked her instantly. Aubrey's parents were more involved with their daughter's dating life than Vic's were with his. He seemed to have no curfews and was able to do what he wanted when he wanted. Which reminded her...

"I should tell my parents I'm not coming home before it gets any later." She leaned off the bed and made a fruitless swipe for her dress. Her cell phone should be in the pocket. She was unsurprised to feel Vic's hands palm her butt while she reached.

"You have the best ass," came his compliment.

"You say that like you're not tired of seeing it yet." Got it! Her hand around the dress, she pulled it into her lap. Vic was lying on his belly, head propped on one fist. She gave his bare butt a light slap. "I like yours, too. Now be quiet so I can tell my parents I've decided to stay."

She pressed a button and commanded, "Call Mom." It rang once, twice, then three times, and she gave up. "They must be at dinner. I'll send a text instead." She kept it simple, typing, Staying with Vic tonight. He'll bring me home in the morning. Good night.

She wrinkled her nose when she tossed her phone onto the bed.

"What is it?" Vic asked.

She folded her legs beneath her. "Why do I feel as if I'm doing something I shouldn't?"

"Because for years you were." He kissed her knee. "You were lying about staying at your friends' houses and I was sneaking you into my room at night."

"It's hard to sneak into a private entrance. Besides, Victor Jr. and Bethany let you do whatever you wanted. I was jealous. My parents are like a pair of hawks. Take this situation, for example. I'm living with them." Which honestly hadn't been *that* bad, but she was tired of rotating the same fifteen articles of clothing. She didn't care what people who favored a capsule wardrobe said, she needed more options. She had a closet full of clothes at home she'd like to utilize. "Maybe you could run me by my apartment before you drop me off in the morning."

"Why?"

"I need a fresh outfit for dinner tomorrow night. I'm tired of wearing the same clothes." She finger-combed her damp hair. "My friends from school invited me to a Tex-Mex taco bar for margaritas. It was Primrose's idea."

Boy, had Aubrey been relieved to know exactly who Primrose was when she'd called. And when the older blonde mentioned that Elise, Hailee, Brooke and Brandie would be joining them, Aubrey had been further relieved to remember each of her coworkers with stark clarity. She called up a mental picture of them easily and remembered what classes they taught without having to think about it.

"How are you getting there? Is your mom going?"

"*No.* I do not need a chaperone."

"What about a driver? I'll take you. I'll sit at the bar and mind my own business."

"Actually, Prim mentioned that Brandie was bringing her new boyfriend, and Brooke was bringing her husband, Kal, so maybe you will have a few dudes to hang out with. If you're sure you're not going to be put out driving me there and back."

"How can I convince you that you're not an inconvenience to me, Aubrey?" He rested his hand on her leg. She had to admit that was nice to hear. She'd felt like an inconvenience since her accident. She'd been the very definition of someone to fret over since she'd been discharged from the hospital.

She squeezed his hand. "I can't tell you how much your support has meant while I'm going through this. Not being able to work has made my days really long. I understand why I never used social media before, but it sure would come in handy when I run out of chores to do with my mother. I swear, that woman never stops cleaning the house. I nearly opened an account out of desperation, but the liability risk is too high. I'd rather not give any of my students' overly involved parents an excuse to complain."

"Impossible. You were teacher of the year. Parents trust you with their trust-fund kids implicitly. And you don't have to stay with your parents indefinitely. You're always welcome here."

"Oh, no, I wouldn't want to be in the way."

"It'd solve your clothing problem, though."

"How?"

"You wouldn't have to wear any if you stayed with me." He flattened her on the bed, rolling onto her and trapping her there with his weight. She closed her eyes and savored everywhere his lips touched, grateful to have him in her life and to be in his.

Vic had never been to Clara's Cantina. He wasn't sure how he'd missed this one—he loved Tex-Mex food. The restaurant was shack-like by design, with cowboy hats hanging from the walls and strings of lights shaped like chili peppers draped across the bar. The vibe was loud and raucous inside, but a bit less so on the open-air veranda where he and Aubrey were headed.

"I can't believe you've never been here," she said as she wove around packed tables, each adorned with baskets of chips and dishes of salsa.

Offering to drive her hadn't been completely altruistic on his part. Her memory loss was still very much a factor, and he couldn't be sure what her friends would say when she brought up her "boyfriend," Vic. She'd mentioned at least one name he recognized from their years in high school together. One friend who would undoubtedly remember when Vic and Aubrey dated, and probably knew they'd broken up as well. Elise and Aubrey had been close back then.

He'd been reminding himself all day that he was simply looking out for Aubrey's health, but if he dug deep, he could admit he was also running interference. He'd made a pretty good case for them living happily ever after, but he wasn't ready for her to learn the whole truth yet—or at least he wanted to be there when she found out.

The five women at the table stood when they spotted Aubrey, clapping their hands and whooping. Diners at surrounding tables glanced over long enough to confirm a celebrity wasn't in their midst, and then returned to their conversations. Then he saw her.

Elise Baxter.

Aubrey was pulled into hug after hug, her friends complimenting her on her outfit or her hair. Elise made a beeline straight for him.

Shorter than Aubrey, Elise stood at a petite five

feet tall, her dark chin-length hair shorter than it had been when they were in high school. Her round, dark brown eyes were narrowed on him, broadcasting her disproval. She'd never liked Vic. He used to believe it was because she was jealous of Aubrey and wanted to date him herself, because of course he had. From the vantage point of a grown man, he recognized his own embarrassing teenage bravado. More likely Elise didn't like him because she'd seen what he hadn't: Aubrey had been too good for him back then.

"What the hell are you doing here?" she snapped.

"Keep your voice down." He smiled for show. Aubrey was chatting with the other ladies, not looking in his direction. "Aub doesn't remember everything about our past. In her mind, we're together."

"In her mind? It looks like you're together in body as well."

"When her memory returns, I will tell her the truth. The doctor doesn't want any sudden memories to ruin the progress she's made."

Elise's eyebrows bent in sympathy. He knew she cared about Aubrey. They all did.

"I'm here because she wants me here," he said. "I'm doing this for her, which is what I'm asking you to do as well." When Elise's features hardened again, he added, "Please?"

She folded her arms over her chest and lifted her chin. "Fine. But if you hurt her again, Grandin, you'll have to deal with me."

"You'll have to stand in line behind her father." He raked a hand through his hair. He was irritated that everyone thought the worst of him, but at the same time he understood why. "For her sake, if you could cover for me if this conversation dips into our relationship, I'd be grateful."

"This is wrong." Elise shook her head but agreed with him when she said, "I'll do it for her."

"Thank you."

She speared him with one final glare before going to give Aubrey a hug and a sunny smile. He did his best to relax, introducing himself to both Brooke's husband, Kal, and Brandie's boyfriend, Roger. Rather than sit next to the two other men, Vic sat next to Aubrey. Something else Elise didn't appear to like.

"Introduce your handsome corn cake, sweetheart," the woman introduced to him as Primrose said in a thick Texas accent. She was broad and blonde, the permanent dimple denting her left cheek making her appear as if she never stopped smiling.

"I've never introduced you to Vic?" Aubrey's eyebrows centered over her nose.

"Of course she has!" Elise interrupted. She turned to Primrose and nodded while she explained, "Remember at the teacher of the year ceremony? We met him that night, some of us for the first time."

"Not Elise." Aubrey shot a thumb over to Vic. "The poor dear had to endure this one in high school."

"Well, you were the poor dear who had to date him." Elise's smile was stiff before she turned back to her friends. "Vic was seated with the principal and his assistant and their spouses. Remember?"

"Oh, of course." Brooke was the first to catch on

to what Elise was trying to do. She jabbed Brandie with an elbow. "We saw so many people that night. Sorry, Vic."

"No big deal."

"How have you been feeling lately?" The woman introduced to him as Hailee directed the question at Aubrey. Her build and clothing style reminded him a bit of Caitlyn Lattimore, his best friend Jayden's sister.

"Better each day," Aubrey answered as she poured herself a margarita from the pitcher at the center of the table. "I still have gaps in my memory, but the doctor is confident they'll return."

"Quite a few gaps," Elise muttered. Vic shot her a warning look.

"Yes, that's true." Aubrey sipped her drink. "This is delicious. Anyway, I've been leaning fairly hard on Vic." She grabbed his hand on the table and squeezed his fingers, looking up at him with trusting eyes. His stomach sank. "He doesn't mind, though."

"I'd do anything for you." He meant it down to his bone marrow. When her memories of the past came back, he'd be there for her. He'd dry her tears or allow her to yell at him. He'd take her fists if she pummeled his chest and declared she hated him for lying to her. He'd defend her parents if needed. He'd drive her to the doctor's office or to dinner with friends or to work and home again once she went back to teaching—anything to prove to her how much he cared.

He'd given up on Aubrey once in his life. He wouldn't do it again.

Fourteen

The next morning, Aubrey and her mother sat on the wide front porch, rocking away on a pair of rockers stationed to the left of the door. Thick green grass stretched alongside the dusty driveway beneath a clear blue sky. It was a perfect day in Royal…almost.

Last night had been fun, more fun than Aubrey had had in a while. She hadn't seen her friends since before the accident, so time with the girls had been good for her heart. After the initial "how are you feeling" questions, everyone had gabbed about work. Having the spotlight off herself and onto what she loved—her job—had been a relief, even if it did make her miss work tenfold. She'd realized then just how exhausting it'd been to solely focus on her injury and healing from it.

Vic had been comfortable and conversational, the perfect foil for her that evening. She didn't feel the need to watch over him or check on him. He'd chatted with the ladies and guys alike. Football or footwear, he'd commented on both topics. More than a few times he'd sent the entire table into fits of laughter. Even Elise had laughed along, and she'd seemed disapproving about him at first. The food had been delicious, authentic Tex-Mex like Aubrey had been raised on, and the margaritas were cool and refreshing.

When Vic had dropped her off at her parents' house after dinner, her face had hurt from smiling. He'd kissed her in his truck and then had kept on kissing her…up until her father turned on the porch light as a nonverbal warning. Vic had commented that he felt like a teenager again, and she'd admitted to feeling the same before climbing out of his truck and going inside.

So, why, after an idyllic evening filled with friends, food, drink and kissing Vic, had Aubrey woken this morning with a tight ball of dread in her stomach? She couldn't understand it.

She'd lain in bed an hour ago, the clean scent of fresh sheets surrounding her, staring at the ceiling. Memories of last night popped into her head one by one, like when Primrose mentioned she hadn't remembered meeting Vic before. Or Elise's insistence that they'd all met him at the awards dinner. And there'd been something about the way her friends had laughed. A little too loud and often, sometimes exchanging glances with each other Aubrey hadn't understood the meaning behind.

She'd ignored the blip of concern in the moment, blaming her lack of social interaction or her uncooperative brain, but by this morning the events of last night had felt...well, *forced.* As if her friends had been performing. She'd told herself she was overreacting, but at the same time, she thought the observation significant.

"Did you and Vic have a nice dinner?" Her mother, a notoriously slow riser, finally spoke, jarring Aubrey out of her hectic thoughts.

"I thought you'd fallen asleep over there."

"Darn near. I had to down half of my coffee before I could form words. How'd I rise and shine back when I taught school? The mind boggles." Her mother shook her head as if amused by her own thoughts. "I miss work sometimes. Gave me something to do with myself."

Mary was a retired English teacher. Aubrey had followed in her mother's footsteps after watching her mother grade papers and read essays by the light of the evening news. Her job had always looked fun to Aubrey.

"We had a nice time. I feel a little off, though. Talking about school and students with my coworkers made me realize how much I miss work." Maybe that's what this bizarre feeling was—her mourning her former routine. Aubrey loved interacting with her students, assigning papers and then reading and grading them. She found ways to encourage and praise every student, no matter what.

When she was younger, she'd pestered her mother with a zillion questions about teaching. She'd shadowed her mother at work for a high school paper. Aubrey had a deep love of learning, so choosing to go to college had been a no-brainer.

She hadn't been ready to marry and start a family at such a young age—not with her entire future up for grabs. No wonder it'd pissed her off when Vic suggested she stay home and have his babies rather than pursue graduate school.

"...you have years and years to teach. Don't worry, you'll be back soon enough," her mother was saying. But Aubrey hadn't been listening for the last several seconds. They'd audibly ticked by alongside each of her heartbeats, which were currently reverberating like a gong in her ears.

What was that thought about Vic and him wanting her to...*have babies instead of going to graduate school?*

She blinked, more confused than when she'd woken up this morning. She couldn't call up a time or place or any snippet of the conversation in her head, but it *felt* real. As real as the rocking chair under her butt and the mug of coffee warming her hands. The feeling of dread returned tenfold. That thought didn't feel like a thought at all. It felt like a *memory*.

"Honey, are you all right?" her mother asked.

"Yes. Yeah." She rubbed her temple where the start of a headache was brewing. "I'm, uh, trying to decide what to do with myself today."

"Lucky for you, I need help reorganizing the bookshelves. You can help me."

"Yes, *so* lucky." Aubrey forced a smile, cupping her mug with both hands to hide the shake in her arms.

She was still wrestling with the off feeling as she finished her coffee and then followed her mother inside. Thirty minutes later, the contents of the massive bookshelf in her mother's office were stacked on the floor and across two desks. Her mother swiped the dust from the top of the shelf and declared it was as clean as it would become. "How about a BLT for lunch? With avocado."

"Sold." Aubrey was hungry after having only coffee for breakfast. "Do you need help?"

"Sure do. Put all of this back for me, will you?" Mary waved in the general direction of the stacks of books, plants and the occasional figurine. Then she walked out, leaving Aubrey to handle the task.

She put away the large books first, mostly hardback coffee-table books about photography and travel. She came across one she recognized, a book about the solar system she'd referenced for her science fair project in her junior year in high school. She'd built a model of the planets, and a darn good one at that. She cracked the spine and found her second-place ribbon wedged between the pages. Gold, not blue like the first-place ribbon had been, but she'd been proud of the win. Vic had told anyone who'd listen that Aubrey should have won, and that Timothy Leighton, who'd won first place, had only claimed first place because he was a kiss-ass.

She smiled at the memory as she continued flipping through the book's pages. Then she came across a long, slender sheet of paper. No, not paper. A strip of photographs. The pictures were of her and Vic at the science fair, from one of those box-shaped, curtain-covered photo booths. In the photos she and Vic were smiling, kissing or pretending to sleep. The bottom one was her favorite. She'd been making a goofy face at the camera, but his eyes had been on her. His expression was raw and beautiful. She could see the love he'd had for her captured in this photo. It radiated even now, as real and alive as it'd ever been.

Or maybe as it used to be.

With a frown, she carefully folded the photo strip in half and tucked it into her back pocket. Her headache had arrived, either from not eating or the bout of overthinking she'd suffered since opening her eyes today. She made quick work of filing the rest of her mother's books and mementos onto the gleaming wood shelves, and then went to join her for lunch.

Vic and Jayden were perched on the fence surrounding the Grandin property, boots hooked on the bottom plank, watching the sun go down on a long day.

Jayden had been Vic's best friend for as long as either of them could remember. Hell, probably since birth. The second-born of the Lattimores, Jayden was wealthy, handsome and Vic's age. Once Vic had been single again, and it'd been clear that Aubrey wasn't changing her mind and coming back to him, Jayden had been there for him. He'd acted as Vic's wingman whenever they'd gone out, and vice versa.

Jayden didn't take life too seriously, which, at the time, had been exactly what Vic had prioritized. Considering a future with anyone other than Aubrey had been too painful—it still was. But what Jayden *did* and had always taken seriously was his family's ranch.

"Alexa is checking in with the PI again," Jayden said, circling back to the topic they always seemed to be talking about lately. The fate of the ranches was still up in the air, and it'd been impossible not to bring it up whenever they were hanging out. Alexa was Jayden's younger sister, and also the family attorney. She had been in direct contact with private investigator Jonas Shaw, who was looking into the issues on the ranch. "Whenever she finds out more, I'll send her over to update you and your family. We're in this together."

"Appreciate it." Vic tipped his can of beer to his lips.

"Hey, what are better-looking best friends for?" Jayden grinned. The asshole. "*Now* are you going to tell me why you're messing with Aubrey Collins, or are we going to pretend that isn't going on?"

"I'm not *messing* with her." Vic heard the defense in his own voice.

"Okay. So you're *not* sleeping with your ex-girlfriend, who doesn't know she's your ex-girlfriend, thanks to a knock on the head?"

"Don't tell me I have to convince you that my motives are pure, too."

"Are they?" Jayden hopped off the fence railing and landed in the grass, then he reclaimed his own beer can that had been resting on the fence post. "What're your plans with her, anyway?"

Vic hopped down as well, one hand in his pocket as he finished off his beer. Jayden didn't want to hear this, but he'd asked, so here went nothing. "I'm winning her back."

His best friend's dark eyebrows shot up. "And when she remembers she hates you, then what?"

"She's changed. *I've* changed. Back when we were arguing over graduate school and whether or not she was ready to be a mother, we were kids ourselves. I know I was an arrogant asshole—"

"Was?" Jayden laughed, then held up a hand. "Last one."

"Yeah, sure." Vic balanced his empty can on the fence post. "Are you honestly telling me you're happy bedding women who don't stick around?"

"Yes." Jayden didn't flinch. "Are you sure you're ready to trade your single status for a woman you haven't been with for a decade? She has a life you know nothing about, Vic. You don't know *each other.* You only know who you used to be. When she remembers she threw the engagement ring at you, she is not going to be happy you have been lying to her this entire time."

"I'm not lying!" Vic shouted. He couldn't frame it that way or he'd lose his mind. "Not really. I'm just… not filling in the gaps. Which her doctor asked me to do, by the way."

"I sincerely doubt her doctor's orders had anything to do with you taking her to bed, or tricking her into falling in love with you before she remembers why she doesn't."

"Dammit, Jayden." Vic didn't know what else to say—probably because what his best friend had said sounded true. And worse, it felt true.

"Look, I'm all for you reconciling with Aubrey. She's great, and she makes you better. You two used to be inseparable. I remember what a miserable jerk you were after she left."

"Thanks a lot," Vic grumbled.

"But," Jayden continued, "this needs to be done under honest pretenses. Tell her the truth. She's strong. She can handle it. The question is, can you?"

"I can handle it," Vic said automatically, though he wondered if he could. Telling her the truth might break her heart and simultaneously land him back in the miserable-jerk stage Jayden had described. "I've given her nothing but solid reasons why we belong together. She'll understand my motives."

"And if she doesn't?"

"I'll convince her. I'm not going to let her walk away this time without her knowing how I feel about her. Life isn't going to work out if we try to find someone else to fall in love with. I've been out there and tried, and I assume she has, too."

"She doesn't remember that, either, I'm guessing. The trying-with-other-people part."

Vic shook his head. "She thinks we've been together nonstop for fourteen years."

It sounded bad when he said it aloud. Like he was trying to manipulate her into being with him. Except for one thing—

"She loves me." Vic watched Jayden's face fall. "She tells me over and over. I want to tell her not to, that she doesn't have to, but..." He rubbed a spot in the center of his chest, the one that had been aching with longing for weeks now. "It feels good, man. It feels really, really good to hear her say that to me again."

Jayden palmed Vic's shoulder in support, his expression broadcasting both sympathy and warning. The man was as close to a brother as Vic had ever had, which was why he would listen to whatever Jayden said next—even if it hurt. By the look on his face, it damn well might.

"It should feel really, really *wrong*. What you and Aubrey have currently has an expiration date. You love her, you want to marry her and walk into forever together, that's fine. I'll be the first in line at the funeral for your single-guy status. But you have to level with her. She deserves not to be the last one to know, Vic. If you love and respect her, *tell her*. Otherwise this ticking time bomb is going to reach zero and then…" Jayden spread his hands and made an exploding sound.

His best friend had put into words everything Vic knew in his heart to be true. His excuses were good ones, arguably honorable. He'd come back into her life—again—for her. To help her through her healing. With a practically clean bill of health, she'd soon be returning to work. He couldn't follow her everywhere she went in case someone told her the truth—he couldn't delay the inevitable. Someone would let slip that Aubrey and Vic hadn't been together for a decade, and then she'd never forgive him.

It was time she learned the truth about what had happened. Even if it meant he would be fighting harder for her than he'd fought before, he would tell her the real reason why her engagement ring was in his dresser drawer.

He'd proposed years ago. She'd chosen not to marry him in the end.

Fifteen

Vic hadn't been this nervous since he'd planned to take Aubrey's virginity—and give up his own—the night of her senior prom. He'd booked a room at a fancy hotel in Dallas and had arranged for strawberries and champagne to be sent to the room. The butterflies in his gut were more like flying dragons when he'd picked her up at her parents' house. He'd been positive Eddie and Mary Collins had seen the sweat on his brow for what it was—not a reaction to the Texas heat, but guilt seeping out of his every pore.

His nerves had given way the moment he and Aubrey had walked into that luxury hotel room. He'd been positive forever was in their future. He'd already purchased an engagement ring with the intention of proposing on her graduation day, which he'd ended up doing. Marriage was inevitable for them, so he saw no reason to wait another minute to actually be with her. She was his destiny, and he'd promised her an evening she'd never forget. Except she *had* forgotten.

Two years after that, he'd made another significant purchase and had planned another surprise for his fiancée. As fate had it, the night he'd tucked a gold key with a red ribbon into his pocket was the same night they'd argued about their future for the final time.

"I'm so tired of your mood swings, Vic Grandin!" Aubrey shouted.

"Keep your voice down."

"Why? Who cares if your sisters overhear? Or your parents. Or everyone in the entire state of Texas!"

"Me!" he shouted back. "I care. And that ring on your finger should make you care. My sisters and parents are about to be your sisters and parents, too."

The argument had been devolving since they'd started. It'd picked up speed since its downhill trajectory, and he'd be damned if he knew how to stop it. Making matters worse, he circled back to the comment that had started this ill-fated conversation.

"Ever since you went off to college you think you're too good to live a lowly life as a Grandin. I could buy you anything you want, and you don't give me credit for that, Aubrey."

"Did it occur to you, golden boy, *that I don't re-*

quire a pampered life? I have wanted to be a teacher since I was a little girl. I want to earn my own money, not have it handed to me."

He ignored the insinuation that he didn't work for his and instead focused on what was really bothering him.

"Becoming a teacher requires the initial bachelor's degree you're in the middle of attaining. Why graduate school? Why extend your college sentence another two or three years? Is the idea of marrying me and starting a family that repulsive?" He was lashing out, and he didn't fully understand why. All he knew was that he'd been ready to marry Aubrey Collins since he'd kissed her for the first time. He'd assumed they'd be married immediately. She'd wanted to wait a few years, and he'd agreed to wait. He'd been patient, and now she wanted to put off the wedding again?

Looking back from an adult standpoint, he understood why he'd lashed out. He'd been hurt. If he'd had a brain cell in his head at the time, he'd have seen that his anger was masking inadequacy he hadn't come to terms with. Instead, he'd yelled and defended himself. Not his finest moment.

"News flash," Aubrey continued. "My going to graduate school has nothing to do with you and everything to do with me and what I want out of life. You're not the only one with aspirations, Victor Grandin the Third*."*

He hated when she called him that. She added "the third" whenever she was upset with him, knowing it upset him. He wasn't a carbon copy of his grandfather and his father. He was the sole male heir in a new generation. He planned on taking the Grandin family ranch to its pinnacle. He'd make his family billions. *History books would rave about how he'd exceeded everyone's expectations. His sisters would finally have to admit he was capable and talented.*

Aubrey folded her arms and pressed her lips together. Her chin quivered and her eyelashes fluttered. He didn't recall having seen her angrier. "Admit it, Vic, we've grown apart."

The accusation hit him like a sucker punch. He blinked away the red in his vision.

"You met someone, didn't you?" he said between clenched teeth. It was the only logical explanation for her not wanting to marry him. "You met an educated guy who wants to be a professor when he grows up, and you believe common interests far outweigh the life a glorified ranch hand could give you. Admit it."

Her mouth fell open. "You have a lot of growing up to do. And yes, that is my college experience talking. If you truly believe I've met someone else while still seeing you, then marrying you is the worst idea I've ever entertained."

Her comment was a dagger straight to his gut. His next words weren't thought out, and they sure as hell weren't kind. "If that's the way you feel, then you shouldn't marry me. You can strut your college-educated ass off my property, but fair warning—if you walk away now, you'll be begging to come back."

She flinched, hurt radiating through her beautiful features, but she shored herself up a second later, tore the engagement ring from her finger and threw it at him. "Fuck you, Vic."

He'd never once heard her drop an F-bomb, so in a way it had been a bomb. The mushroom cloud had hovered over his head as she stomped to her car. He'd followed her, shouting as she drove off that she'd come crawling back to him. He'd promised her he'd be counting down the hours until she returned.

Shame coated him as he remembered that night in graphic detail. It was like it'd been tattooed onto his skin. He'd been an entitled, arrogant asshole at the end. Was it any wonder why she'd never spoken to him again? It'd been a miracle she'd agreed to go to bed with him the night he'd bought her a drink at the Silver Saddle. It'd taken some balls to ask her for more after having been so shallow.

Hands gripping the steering wheel of his truck, he surfaced from the bad memories and focused on the road. His Aubrey with the auburn hair sat next to him, singing the words to a song on the radio. How did she remember lyrics but not one of the most significant memories from her past? In a way, it would have been easier if she'd remembered on her own—preferably during one of the nights she'd spent at his house. Then he could've held her close and explained how this was their second chance. He'd remind her that she'd been the one who asked for him after the accident—didn't that count for something?

She shut off the radio when the song ended. "How much longer?"

Excitement danced in her eyes. He'd wanted to kiss her since he'd picked her up but had resisted.

He had no right to take anything more from her. Not until she knew the whole truth.

Permission had come via her parents, who had spoken to Aubrey's doctor. He'd confessed to Mary and Eddie that he couldn't spend another moment keeping Aubrey in the dark. He loved her but couldn't tell her. Not when she didn't fully understand the circumstance. He'd expected a fight, but her parents had agreed. Her doctor gave the green light. Aubrey was ready.

Vic sure as hell wasn't.

During their drive, she'd mentioned that she'd been feeling unsettled lately. He pressed gently, asking her why. She'd shared that she'd felt confused, and he'd promised she wouldn't be confused after today. And then he told her he had a surprise for her.

"It's just up the road," he answered as he drove closer to their destination.

"Are you sharing what it is, or do I have to wait?"

She loved surprises. She loved him. After she learned the truth, would she still?

He held her hand while navigating through a posh neighborhood lined with large houses. "Does any of this look familiar?"

Outside her window was a landscape of lush green lawns, blooming flowers and fall decorations on porches.

"Yes." She gasped. "This *is* familiar. We've driven through this neighborhood before, haven't we? It feels like it's been a while."

"It's been a long while. Over a decade." His spine stiffened as he slowed down. They were close. "We used to pretend we were shopping for our dream home. You picked your favorite, I picked mine."

"And they were the same one!" She laughed. "Oh my God, I remember! It was a transitional style, brick and stone. Two-car garage. Do you have any idea how good it feels to remember? So good."

He hoped her excitement held through what he'd brought her here to tell her.

He presented his ID at the gate separating a ritzier part of the neighborhood from the one behind them and then drove the short distance to the house she'd described.

"Vic? What is this?" she asked when he pulled into the driveway. He'd had the interlocked paverstone driveway laid two years ago.

"I bought the house. I never told you." When she gawped at him, he gave her a tentative smile. "Surprise."

The tears came as another laugh stuttered from her lips. "You're serious."

"Yep. Hop out and I'll show you the inside."

As he slipped the key into the dead bolt, she hugged him from the side. He turned to embrace her, holding her tight and never wanting to let her go. Would she be this happy a few minutes from now? He doubted it.

He unlocked the door and ushered her in ahead of him. They stood at the base of a long foyer, which led to the rest of an unfurnished home. To their right was a living room with built-in bookshelves, ideal for housing Aubrey's massive book collection. To their left, a dining room large enough to host both his family and hers for Thanksgiving or Christmas dinners. He took her hand and led her through the arched foyer to the stairway leading upstairs.

There wasn't a speck of dust in the place, thanks to the cleaning crew he'd hired. During the anger stage of their breakup, he'd been convinced he'd move into this house one day, and then she'd regret leaving him when she saw what she'd missed out on. When he'd hit the grieving stage, he'd kept the house up in case a miracle occurred and she came back to him. After that, well, he hadn't needed a reason. Maintaining the house had become habit, and the idea of letting it go felt like a death. He'd revisited the notion of moving in here himself but ultimately hadn't been able to stomach it. Even though she'd never stepped foot inside, he saw Aubrey in every corner and crevice.

"This is incredible. I can't believe you did this! How soon can we move in?" Her hopeful expression was too much to take. What he wouldn't give for them to be this way forever. Excitedly building a life together, piece by piece, no gap in her memories of them being together to worry about. From the start, he'd known it would be a bad idea to lie to her. He'd vowed to do what was best for her, but somehow that had become lost in what was best for him. He prayed she could forgive him—and find enough good reasons to stay with him after he told her the truth.

"How many bedrooms?" Her voice bounced off the walls and ceiling as she craned her head to look up at the second floor.

"Four bedrooms. Three and a half bathrooms." He'd figured they'd have at least three children, so the house would hold them for a while. "Before we talk about, ah, moving in, I have something to tell you. Would you like to sit down?"

Her excitement morphed into worry as she chewed on the inside of her lip. "Is it bad?"

"Not…exactly."

"If it's bad news, and it feels like it might be, say it fast."

He'd had an idea of what he wanted to say since the night he'd talked to Jayden, but he hadn't decided in what order to say it.

"Oh my God." She put her hand over her heart. "You're breaking up with me, aren't you?"

"What? No. Aub, that's the last thing I want. I—Listen. Can you not talk until I'm finished? I have a lot to say."

She nodded and then walked up a few stairs. Lowering onto the third step, she rested her elbows on her knees and pressed her folded hands to her mouth. Then, she waited.

Fuck. He didn't want to do this. He didn't want to look into the eyes of the woman he loved and tell her he'd kept a very big, very important secret from her. But he owed her the truth.

No matter how badly she took it.

Sixteen

Vic paced the floor in front of her for the count of ten. He stopped in front of her, put his hands on his hips and looked her dead in the eye. Then he said the last thing in the world she expected him to say.

"We haven't been a couple for ten years."

She opened her mouth to ask what the hell he was talking about, but he lifted his hand to stay her interruption.

"In fact, we've barely spoken during the last ten years." He pushed a hand through his hair and watched her carefully.

What followed were a number of things that sounded foreign but *felt* true. He mentioned proposing to her at her graduation party in front of her family. She immediately called up the exact spot in her parents' house where she'd been standing. He brought up the time they'd argued about her going to graduate school, which matched the random memory she'd had the other morning. And, finally, he slid together the pieces of the night they'd shared before her accident.

"At the bar, I asked you to come home with me for old times' sake. I promised to make you forget your name. I swore you'd never have to see me again after if you said yes to one last time." He swallowed thickly, the picture of remorse, while her blood pressure rose higher and higher. "You forgot that part, believing instead that us sleeping together was evidence that I was currently in your life. But I wasn't, Aubrey. Not before that night."

"We shared cannoli," she said, the words sounding like they were coming from someone else. She pictured him that night, smug and grinning, offering her a cherry stem he'd tied into a knot with his tongue. The edges of that memory were sharp and clear, in full focus for the first time since her accident. He'd promised her a wicked, delicious time in the sack. She'd forgotten that part until now. She'd forgotten how he'd charmed his way into her pants.

Anger pushed her to her feet like a shot. She was surprised she didn't go rocketing straight through the roof.

"You fell the next day," he continued, hands out as if begging her to hear him out. "Your parents tried to keep me away, but I was at the hospital, in the waiting room, the entire time. I swore not to leave until they let me see you. Your doctor agreed it was a good idea to bring me back into your life. At least until your memory returned."

She let out a humorless laugh. "You all lied to me."

"Your doctor was worried that if your memory returned too fast, you'd suffer a setback. None of us wanted that. We could have lost you once, and we weren't willing to risk it again."

His tender tone wasn't comforting her, it was *infuriating* her.

"I stopped by your parents' house a few days ago, when you went shopping with Elise. I told them I couldn't keep this from you any longer. Your mom called your doctor and explained the situation. Everyone agreed it was the right time for you to know the truth."

"Everyone except for me. Also, I'm questioning the validity of my doctor's medical degree right about now."

"I never meant to hurt you, Aub. I was trying to help."

"You strung me along. You treated me to dinners and dates. You took me to bed." Her voice shook in a way that scared her. Had she ever been this angry in her life? But then she recalled, vividly, the moment she'd unceremoniously returned Vic's engagement ring and decided that yes, once before, she'd been this goddamn angry. "You let me believe in a future for us when you had no intention..." Her voice trailed off as she backed away from him, thoroughly disgusted.

"I didn't intend for it to go this far, I swear. I thought—"

"I told you I loved you." She swept her hair behind her ears while staring at him in disbelief. Could she have been stupider? "You let me believe we were in love this entire time."

"We were. We *are*." He took a step closer to her, but she lifted an arm, warning him not to come closer. "I told your parents how much I love you. I still love you, Aub. I never stopped. If it hadn't been for your accident, we might never have had a second chance."

"A second chance?" Memories flooded over her like a bucket of ice water. She remembered. She remembered *everything*. The proposal. Showing off the ring to friends and family. Her decision to attend graduate school and the argument that followed.

"You told me I'd come crawling back."

"Aubrey—"

"Was this a twisted revenge plot? Were you retaliating because I broke your precious pride? Did you buy this house out of spite? Did you bring me here to show me what I could have if I allow you back into my life?"

He opened his mouth to respond, but she kept right on talking.

"You accused me of cheating on you with a faceless, nameless college guy."

"I asked. I didn't accuse."

"Same thing."

"Can you— For just a second, can you imagine what it was like for me back then? How hurt I was hearing you didn't want to marry me?"

"Oh, are you the victim here? I'm sorry. Here I thought I was the one with a traumatic brain injury causing me to forget *the most important part of my life*!" She was yelling now, and forced to grip her head as pain shot through both temples. There was too much to process. Too many old memories to reconcile with the new.

They came in tsunami form, laying waste to everything she thought she knew to be true. The idea of marrying Vic, destroyed. Her steadfast trust in him, demolished. The love she'd felt for him, washed away.

"Please, Aubrey."

"No. You have one final task on your Aubrey to-do list, and that's to drive me to my parents' house. On the way, I don't want to hear anything you have to say. You owe me at least that."

He watched her for the count of five before agreeing with a nod. He gestured to the front door. She kept her eyes on the exit rather than admiring the house as she left it—a house she'd never live in. She kept her head down when she walked past the freshly mown lawn. A lawn her future children would never play on.

She'd lost her future with Vic in one fell swoop, and he had been the one who'd taken it from her. The worst part about it was knowing he'd betrayed her not once, but *twice*.

There wouldn't be a third.

Vic didn't speak during the drive back to her parents' house. Not until he parked in the driveway. "Can I—"

"No. No to whatever it is you're going to ask." A tremor of regret slipped down her spine at his sincere expression. She shook it off. He'd lied to her for too long. She wasn't going to give him the chance to explain his way out of it—or *buy* his way out of it by offering her a dream home. "No to living with you. No to marrying you. No to you ever touching me again. In fact, I don't want to speak to you again. We have nothing left to say to each other."

She hopped out and slammed the truck door, the aggressive action renewing her strength. He sat in his truck in the driveway, engine idling. He could sit there until the cows literally came home. She meant every word of what she'd said.

"Mom! Dad!" She threw open the door and tossed her purse onto the kitchen counter.

Her parents were in the living room, books open on their laps. Her father blinked as if he'd just woken from a nap. He slid his glasses onto his nose.

"How could you betray me like that?" she asked them both. "How could you let me believe that Vic was a part of my life?"

"Now, honey, calm down." Her father set his book aside.

"Not going to happen." She turned to her mother. "You had plenty of opportunities to tell me the truth. I thought we were growing closer. And you—" she pointed at her father "—you have always protected me. Did you decide there was a time limit on safe-guarding your daughter?"

"We were following your doctor's—" he started.

"Orders. I've heard, I've heard. I'm going to pay her a visit next. I'm going to drive myself there. She was worried about me driving, but tumbling into bed with my ex-boyfriend was well within the confines of her Hippocratic oath."

"Dr. Mitchell explained her concerns in detail. The human brain is a complicated web of—"

"Daddy! Seriously. Stop."

He did, his shoulders sagging under the weight of what Aubrey could only guess was guilt. "I'm sorry. We're both so damn sorry. We made a mistake because we were trying to protect you. We love you so much."

"You should have seen Vic when he was here," her mother interjected. "He was truly agonized. Practically in tears when he confessed he was in love with you. He said he wanted more than anything to win you back. He begged us to let him tell you the truth himself. He's taken on the blame, but it's not his fault. We had hoped him being back in your life would give you a safe place to land while your memory returned. You were so happy whenever he was around."

She tried not to let the words penetrate, but picturing Vic here, his heart on his sleeve, cut her to the core. The man she had spent the last month believing she loved was a different version than the man she'd driven away from ten years ago. That night she'd broken his heart and hers. She'd cried and cried, stubborn tears she'd believed might never dry.

But they had.

They had dried, and then she'd made the epically stupid decision to go to bed with Vic because he'd been charming and offered her a knotted cherry stem. But she'd made a life for herself without him.

It was a good life. One without regrets. It could have stayed that way, too, if he hadn't come along and shown her a glimpse of the life she'd lost out on. Including the dream home they'd imagined moving into when they were younger.

That bastard. He'd used the best part of her—her trusting heart—against her. She'd never forgive him. "Vic and I have issues that are our own and none of your damn business."

"Like it or not," her mother replied, "you were happier before you knew the truth."

"Ignorance is bliss, Mom? Really? Any happiness you thought you saw was a fabrication. It was based on the fairy tale you were allowing me to believe."

"Darling, we love you," her mother continued.

"I know you do." Her voice wobbled with unspent emotion. Anger and sadness, regret and heartbreak warred for first place. "I suspect Vic believes he means it when he says it, too. That's not what's up for debate. The question is how will I choose to move forward now that I have the complete information. Only I can make that decision. And I have." She swung to face her father, adding, "I've decided to move out immediately. I'm going to return to my apartment, and I'll let you know when *or if* you're allowed to see me again. You're both going to respect my privacy. Like I told Vic, it's the least you can do."

Her piece said, she stormed to her borrowed bedroom and slammed the door. She flipped the lock, yanked her suitcases out of the closet and began packing her clothes. While she did, she cried.

She cried out of grief at Vic's and her parents' betrayal. She cried out of joy for her regained memory. And she cried out of sadness, because the ugly truth was that she *did* love Vic.

She loved him more than she should, especially knowing that he'd kept her in the dark about their past. A tiny voice in the back of her mind asked what else he'd been lying to her about.

Could she trust the man she'd spent the last several weeks with? Or had he been charming her for his own gain, much like he had the night at the Silver Saddle?

Seventeen

Vic had stuck around the Collins house after Aubrey slammed his truck's door. He'd sat in their driveway, debating whether or not to knock on the door and then further debating how long to give Aubrey to tell her parents off before he knocked on the door.

He'd settled on twenty minutes. It'd been Eddie who'd answered. Mary had been at the kitchen table, wadded tissues in her hands, eyes red.

"Hey, Vic," Eddie had said mildly. Which had been ever so slightly alarming, as Eddie rarely greeted Vic with anything less than disdain. "Come on in."

"Is she all right?" Vic stepped inside, surprised when Mary came to him for a quick hug. When she'd patted him on the back in a motherly fashion, a torrent of emotion hammered him. Once upon a time, these people had been his future in-laws.

"It's not your fault," she'd assured him. "It's ours. She's upset. She'll be all right."

Mary hadn't looked as if she believed herself, but Vic could tell she was trying to be strong for him, the man who'd let this mess go on far longer than he should have.

Eddie had told him that Aubrey was packing and that he planned on taking her back to her apartment. "I know my daughter. She needs time to process. She needs to be alone for a while."

"I'd offer to help, but..." Vic had shrugged, feeling useless. Eddie had shaken his head, silently confirming it'd be a bad idea to offer.

That was five days ago.

Five days was as long as Vic was willing to wait before he went to see Aubrey. His texts had gone unanswered. He didn't bother calling her in case she was pissed off enough to block his number. He'd sent flowers, but anonymously. Who knew what she'd done with them. No doubt she'd figured out they were from him.

At her apartment door, he steeled himself for rejection, no matter what form it took. Whether she screamed at him or slapped him, he'd weather her storm. He'd do it for her—because he loved her.

He rolled his shoulders, looked up and down the quiet hallway and then knocked lightly. He wished he knew where her head was at. It'd help to know if she was crying or—

The door swung aside, and she stood there, jaw

squared, head cocked as if daring him to speak. She wore flat white tennis shoes and a floral dress that hugged her subtle curves. She was at once the sexy, strong-willed woman who'd talked him into sleeping with her and the vulnerable woman he hadn't meant to take advantage of.

She wasn't smiling. He wondered if she'd ever smile at him again.

"Yes?" she clipped.

"Five minutes." She began closing the door. He stopped it with his hand and sought her emerald eyes for any sign that the Aubrey who loved him was still in there. "Two minutes?"

Her features softened briefly before she opened the door and invited him in. She shut it with a snap.

"You kept them." A vase of wildflowers stood in the center of her kitchen table. His heart buoyed. Maybe she didn't hate him.

"It would've been wasteful to throw them out. Even if they are from the man I never want to speak to again."

"You're speaking to me now."

"What are you doing here?"

Right to the point. Still, he couldn't help delaying the inevitable.

"You have a nice apartment." He wandered from the kitchen, painted sunny yellow, to the vibrant turquoise-and-white living room. Red throw pillows decorated a futon, and a bookshelf in one corner was overflowing with books. He thought of the bookshelves in their dream home. Of how living there with her seemed even further away than it had the first time she'd left him. "The last time I was here, I didn't really look around."

"You have one minute left," she reminded him tersely.

"Letting you go was the biggest mistake I ever made," he blurted. He was out of time and out of excuses. She needed to hear the raw truth, and if she was granting him a minute to say it, he was going to use every second. "The day we fought over you continuing college, and delaying the wedding… I have no excuse for my behavior except that I was an entitled twenty-one-year-old jackass."

She inclined her chin in agreement.

"I was angry with you at first. I kept telling myself I deserved better. That if you loved me, you'd marry me right away, school or no school. But hear me, Aub. I was the one who pushed you away. A few years later, I accepted that I'd blown it. I wanted to call and check on you, but I didn't. At one point, I bumped into your dad at an event in town. He told me you had a boyfriend. Hearing that wrecked me. Just split me in two. I decided I was going to get over you, finally, and rid myself of the pain. Then the grief came. It stayed a hell of a lot longer than the anger."

Her eyebrows bowed in sympathy, but her body language was closed. Feet together. Arms crossed. Lips pressed into a flat line. He'd known this wasn't going to be easy. Hell, he didn't deserve for her to make it easy on him. Years ago, he'd stubbornly believed that if he told her to leave, she'd come back. Instead, he'd altered the course of both their lives.

"When I heard your voice over my shoulder that

night at the Silver Saddle, I would have done anything to convince you to have a drink with me. It was my last shot, or so I thought. A Hail Mary that never should have worked. But then you said yes. It was a miracle."

"It was a weak moment."

"It was a weak moment for me, too. Believe me." If he'd have let her walk out of the tapas bar—if she'd never spotted him sitting there—he could have spared his heart shattering all over again. "I never dreamed we'd have a second chance. One night, sure, but I knew the morning I walked out of your bedroom that was it. Then, after your fall, you were asking for me and—"

"All your dreams came true?"

He blew out a breath. He understood why she was upset. But she was still listening, so he tried again.

"Since that night we slept together—the night you had your memory," he added, watching as her cheeks tinged pink with either embarrassment or anger, "I knew I couldn't leave you alone like I promised. I didn't have a plan, but I figured we'd run into each other here and there at the club. I'd hoped I could build on that great night, and you could learn to trust me again. The accident was as unexpected as you asking for me when you woke up. I didn't want to lie to you, but you were just so…" He lifted a hand and dropped it "…*you*. And you were looking at me like you used to and…" He blew out a breath. "God, I couldn't say no to you. I've never been so undeserving. I know that. But I decided to show you how I'd changed. I decided to prove to you how much you mean to me. I'd hoped, once your memory returned, that you could find it in your heart to forgive me. I'm still hoping that. I swear, Aub, I'll never lie to you again."

"Damn straight you won't," she said, but her voice had gone quiet and her arms had loosened from their position over her chest.

Had she forgiven him? If he took a step toward her, would she accept him in her arms?

"I never stopped loving you." His words laid him bare, and for the first time he related to the vulnerability Aubrey had been feeling lately. "Through the angry times and the grieving times, and the apathy that ate up most of my twenties. I know what I did was unfair to you. But you have to believe me when I tell you it came from a genuinely good place. I wasn't exacting revenge when I took you up to that loft, or watched the sunset with you, or showed you our dream home. I was falling in love with you. Again."

He pulled the velvet box holding her engagement ring from his jeans pocket and set it on her kitchen counter. Her eyes widened, her head already shaking back and forth.

"Don't say anything yet. Please. I want you to know I'd marry you in a heartbeat if you'd take me back. If you don't..." His heart splintered at the possibility. "If you don't, you should keep the ring. Like my heart, it was always yours."

She didn't cry or shout. She didn't accuse him of playing her or open her arms for a hug. She stood stock-still, her face blank, unreadable. When she opened her mouth, he had no idea what she'd say.

"Time's up."

...but it sure as fuck wasn't that.

Aubrey pulled open her apartment door, the action echoing her sincerity. She wanted him to leave. He would leave.

In the hallway, however, he couldn't help turning around. He barely managed to say, "You know where to find me," before she shut the door in his face.

The next evening, Vic was mucking Titan's stall when Morgan came trotting up to the stable on a chestnut mare.

"I didn't know you were here," he said in greeting. He'd been in his own head a lot lately, which was the reason he was out here laboring. The busier his hands, the quieter his mind.

"It's a beautiful night. I couldn't resist a ride. Why are you still working?" His sister climbed off the horse.

He shrugged, not wanting to share, well, anything. She didn't let him off the hook.

"You forget, Vic, I know you. Your sad expression says it all."

"I'm not sad," he snapped. Which wasn't true. He was so sad, he might as well be wearing the emotion like a fluorescent-pink bunny costume.

He took the wheelbarrow by the handles, intending to put distance between himself and Morgan, and any talk of what was festering inside him, but his overly involved sister moved to block his path. "Hey, talk to me."

Resigned, because Morgan could and would dig

in if he didn't tell her something, he set the wheelbarrow down. It was hot this evening. He pulled off his gloves and swiped the sweat from his brow. "You have nothing to worry about. I'm not interested in talking with any more women this week, given the way my last conversation went."

Morgan cocked her head. "You went to see her, didn't you?"

"Went to see her, told her the truth. Confessed that I never stopped loving her and left the engagement ring on her kitchen counter." He shrugged, but he felt nowhere near that casual. He felt like a pile of glass shards. In a word, *broken.* And he had no one to blame but himself. "She kicked me out."

"Oh, Vic." Morgan slung both arms around his neck, and those glass shards splintered into smaller pieces and cut deeper. She gave him a squeeze. "Are you going to be okay?"

He gave her a light squeeze in return and cleared his suspiciously full throat. "Of course."

"It's a lot," she continued. "What you're going through. With the ranch drama and reuniting with Aubrey. We knew her finding out the truth was an inevitability, but I'd hoped she'd see you had the best intentions."

"Me, too," he croaked. It hadn't worked out that way, though.

"You know I'm here for you. I love you, big brother."

"I love you, too." Morgan was the best. It hurt to smile, if that's what he was doing. He might be grimacing for all he knew.

"Is that Alexa?" Morgan gestured to the driveway. Vic looked over his shoulder at the car he hadn't noticed as Chelsea and Layla exited the front door of the ranch house.

Jayden's sister–slash–attorney-at-law climbed from her vehicle to greet the other two women, and then the three of them headed in Vic and Morgan's direction.

"Do you think it's good news?" Morgan asked him.

"The way my week's going?" he mumbled. "I doubt it."

"I told you she was a good girl, didn't I, Morg?" Layla called out as she approached. She took the mare's reins in hand as soon as she was close enough.

"You never miss a chance to smell like a horse," Alexa teased Layla as she pulled the sunglasses off her nose.

"Never," Layla agreed with her best friend before planting a smacking kiss on the horse's muzzle.

"You look awful," Chelsea told Vic.

"He's fine," Morgan snapped before turning to Alexa and complimenting her outfit. Ever the city girl at heart, Alexa's jeans and shirt were crisp and pressed.

"So?" Chelsea prompted their visitor.

Alexa got right to the point. "There's been a new development."

Vic didn't have to look at his siblings to know he wasn't the only one whose ears had perked.

Alexa recapped what they'd learned about the surveyor Vic had seen on the property. Her name was Ruby. She'd been hired by Heath—nothing new there.

Vic braced for bad news to follow. That seemed par for the course. Bad news on top of bad news, and then to the left of that, oh, look…more bad news.

Alexa leveled him with a sharp look. "I spoke with Jonas Shaw and asked for an update. He finally touched base with Sylvia."

"Sylvia, as in your grandfather's retired secretary," Layla said, her eyebrows lifting meaningfully.

"One and the same. She wrapped up her wilderness trek and reached out to the investigator. She had plenty to say. It won't come as a surprise to you all to hear she confirmed that my grandfather Augustus and your grandfather Victor Senior were as thick as thieves."

"Tell us something we don't know," Chelsea said.

"Okay, I will." Alexa tucked a lock of hair behind her ear. "Sylvia also mentioned an oil survey done the year before our grandfathers signed over the rights to Cynthia."

Cynthia, as in Heath and Nolan Thurston's mother. After Cynthia and her daughter, Ashley, had subsequently died, Heath had taken it upon himself to stir up trouble. Vic could understand acting out of grief to avenge his family, but the damage he was causing was unforgivable. The ranch was more to the Lattimores and Grandins than a chunk of land to fight over in court.

"There's no proof of oil on this land," Chelsea said.

"Which I'm sure is why the surveyor was poking around your property and ours," Alexa said. "Sylvia swears there was an oil survey done in the past. According to her, the results were clear. There was never oil on this land."

"That's great," Vic said, not trusting the relief in his voice.

"Not so fast." Alexa held up a hand. "Sylvia can't confirm it without paperwork. She went so far as to suggest the purported oil rights were given to Cynthia to keep her quiet."

"Like hush money?" Morgan asked.

"What better way to keep the pregnancy quiet?" Alexa said.

Layla snorted. "It's beginning to sound like Ashley Thurston was Uncle Daniel's daughter after all."

"The timing works," Alexa admitted, "but without DNA, we can't know for sure. The PI told me he was getting in touch with the surveyor Sylvia told him about, in the hopes of uncovering the original paperwork. We know his name's Harry Lawrence and that he lives outside Houston. If he's the stickler for record-keeping Sylvia swears he is, it's only a matter of time before we know the truth."

"What a mess," Vic grumbled, eyes on the pile of shit he'd mucked from Titan's stall. What an apt metaphor for his life right now. If that survey existed, it would prove whether or not there was oil on the land. If there was oil, hell…

Vic didn't want to think about what might happen next.

Eighteen

Aubrey had angry-cleaned her apartment so many times, a speck of dust wouldn't dare settle onto a surface without her express permission.

She'd scheduled a visit with her doctor this afternoon. To her credit, Dr. Mitchell had apologized for any consequential turmoil that had come as a result of Aubrey's treatment plan. She'd explained her reasoning, which had involved another patient having a massive lapse and requiring further hospitalization after well-meaning family members and friends told her everything about her past.

Aubrey didn't wholly agree with her doctor's choices, but she understood why her parents had tried to protect her. They'd been frightened and worried. Involving Vic had gone too far, though, and she hadn't quite forgiven them for it yet.

The bottom line was that Aubrey's memory was back. Dr. Mitchell assured Aubrey that she could continue living her life as she had before her fall, as long as she introduced each piece gradually. She'd informed her well-meaning doctor that the Vic piece would not be introduced again.

She drove—herself, thank you very much—to lunch for a Reuben sandwich with french fries. She'd called her principal on the way to ask how soon she could return to work. Thankfully the answer was "Monday," and her principal assured her she'd be welcomed back with open arms. It was the good news she'd needed to hear.

She was excited to return to her classroom and to the students she'd missed so much. She was also looking forward to having a schedule she created herself, without parameters.

At an outdoor table at the restaurant, she was scribbling her work schedule into her pocket calendar when a familiar voice said her name. She looked up to find Chelsea Grandin, wearing slim-fitting jeans, a flannel and a pair of dark sunglasses, standing over her.

"Chelsea. Hi." She resisted tacking on *How odd to see you here.*

"May I?" The other woman's smile was friendly as she gestured to the empty chair.

"Sure." Just when Aubrey had convinced herself running into Vic's oldest sister was a coincidence, Chelsea laid waste to that idea.

"You're a hard woman to find." She pushed her sunglasses into her dark hair and ordered an iced tea from the waiter. "It's a hot one today. I figured you were either at home or with your parents, but you weren't at your apartment when I stopped by, and a phone call confirmed you weren't speaking to your mom and dad any longer."

Aubrey's heart crushed as she pictured her mother disclosing that fact. Even so, she managed, "That's hardly any of your business, Chelsea."

"I know. I'm meddling." She waved a hand. "I was ready to give up, but then I saw your red hair gleaming from this very patio."

The waiter approached and asked if they were ready to order. Aubrey ordered her Reuben, and Chelsea ordered the same.

"Why are you searching for me? Did you want to congratulate me on my wise decision to never speak to your brother again?"

Chelsea's features softened. "No. The opposite."

The hurt in her expression reminded Aubrey of the day Vic had come over and said the most beautiful words he'd ever said to her. Words that, unfortunately, had come too late. Words she'd tried to convince herself meant nothing. Words that had taken hold of a tiny part of her, but she refused to give them access to the rest of her.

"He's different from the boy you remember, Aubrey."

Voice hard, Aubrey replied, "I remember everything."

"Yes, but you broke up with a different guy than

you've been dating. Vic is..." His sister lifted her hand and dropped it on the table. "My God, he used to be my nemesis. He has been a burr in my ass for as long as I can remember. Cocky. Headstrong. Entitled. I never knew what you saw in him back then. You were, and still are, a strong woman with your own ideas. From where I was standing, it seemed like he was trying to cram you into his mold."

Aubrey agreed with every word of that, so she sat straighter, feeling seen for the first time.

"But when you came back—" Chelsea's wide smile reappeared. "He was different with you. He was different with *me*. With Layla. With everyone. You unlocked a part of his heart no one could reach. A part that never would have been accessible if you didn't break up with him in the first place. Don't you see, Aubrey? Even if you never take him back, he's better for having had you in his life. That change will last forever."

Aubrey wasn't sure what to do with that information.

"I hear he gave you a ring."

"He left it on my kitchen counter." She'd stashed it in her dresser drawer. "I intend on returning it. If you want to follow me back to my apartment, I can give it to you and—"

"No way." Chelsea held up both hands. "I don't blame you for being upset with him. You feel betrayed. And probably overwhelmed. But if you think back on the days you spent with Vic recently, and the feelings you've had for him for years, you might realize you still love him. If that's the case, then, well, you two might have a shot at making this work."

"Did he tell you about the house?" Aubrey asked, anxious to move this conversation along and not dwell on the *L* word Chelsea had brought up.

"What house?"

Aubrey detailed the neighborhood they used to drive through when they'd been teenagers, dreaming of the house they'd move into when they were married. Then she dropped the bombshell. "He bought it. For us. He's kept it up for ten years."

"Seriously?" His sister appeared shell-shocked. "I always assumed he had an apartment in town, but he's been staying in a house?"

"No. It's empty." Aubrey's voice cracked. Telling Chelsea about the house was supposed to serve as proof of the ultimate betrayal: Vic attempting to gift her a house to cover for his lies. But as she described him bringing her there, and how he'd shared that he'd let it sit unoccupied for a decade, it didn't sound like a betrayal. It sounded almost...romantic.

"I can only imagine what you must be thinking right now," Chelsea said, "but that is Vic saying *I love you* in big bold letters. Ten years he's been hiding this? I have given him so much hell about moving out and being the man of his own house. How did he keep this from everyone for so long?"

"He brought me there to break the worst news of my life to me," Aubrey continued, stubbornly not wanting to give him the benefit of the doubt. Her heart was raw, and her recently returned memory was smarting like a fresh cut. "Who knows how many other women he's brought there?"

But she knew. *None.* It wasn't his style. Vic had been heartbroken when he'd shown Aubrey the house—more so by the time she'd walked out of it.

"He brought you there, to the home you'd always wanted, to break your fall, sweetheart. You might not want to see it that way, but I know my brother. I know he loved you more than anything in the world when we were kids, and I know he's lost without you now. I don't want you to feel sorry for him, or make a rash decision because I'm taking his side. I want you to evaluate your own feelings and trust them."

"How can I trust them when I couldn't trust myself for the last six weeks?" And that was the real issue, wasn't it? Aubrey had been her own guiding light for a good ten years, and then suddenly she hadn't been able to count on herself for anything. What she'd felt while with Vic had *seemed* real. But was it? Should she trust the way she'd felt then or the way she was feeling now?

"You're going to have to learn." Chelsea put her hand over Aubrey's and in a stern, oldest-sister-knows-best tone added, "You are strong. You always have been. You know what you want out of life, and you aren't afraid to say what it is. I'm asking you to entertain the idea that Vic could be part of your future. What if you miss the opportunity for a second chance?"

"You sound like him. I was injured, and he took advantage of my weakness." How come no one understood that?

"Then why did you wake up after your accident asking for my brother? Why did him showing up to your hospital room change everything for you? What was the last memory you had of him? The Vic who you fought with and left years ago, or the Vic who went out of his way to show you how much he cares about you?"

Chelsea let the question hang. Their sandwiches were delivered. Aubrey didn't answer as she picked at her food. She didn't want to admit that the last memory she'd had of Vic when she woke up after her accident was the incredible night she'd spent with him.

"Why don't you let me buy you a drink? You can eat your cannoli here. I promise I'll be nice."

"Nice *is not a description of Vic Grandin one hears very often."*

He'd persisted that night and had talked her into sleeping with him. It should have been a ludicrous idea—one she never should have considered.

Why did *you consider it?*

An excellent question.

The answer was as complicated and as simple as the fact that she'd simply wanted to experience him again. Experience his smile, his dark eyes on hers. Taste his mouth and feel safe and protected by his strength. Relax knowing the man in her bed would deliver a beautiful night to remember.

Only she'd forgotten the most important part. She'd forgotten his promise to go away after the sex. A promise he'd broken…

But you broke it first.

She stared at her plate, her thoughts dipping and

swirling. Not because she'd forgotten why she'd said yes, but because she *remembered.* She remembered the intensity of being in bed with Vic. He'd consumed her that night. He'd been so present and real and perfect. She'd done her level best to keep her walls up, but if she were being honest, she'd been sad when he'd left the following morning. Sad about them not having another night in their future. When she'd seen him at the TCC pool party that afternoon, it'd been Vic who'd offered a smile and a polite nod hello. He hadn't approached her, instead giving her ample room to kick the crack in the door wider. In spite of wanting him again—very badly—she'd reached for the handle and pulled it closed instead.

She'd been protecting herself. Then, and now.

When she'd woken up in the hospital asking for Vic, part of her must have wanted the strength and security he offered. So much so that she'd pushed away any memories that hadn't fed that narrative. Her subconscious had lied to her. A coconspirator to Vic, unbeknownst to her.

"Aubrey? Are you okay?" Chelsea asked.

"So much has happened since the day Vic and I broke up. I moved on. I dated other people. He dated other people."

Chelsea's lips flattened before she said, "I don't see either of you with other people now."

"A lot has happened since I was twenty," Aubrey whispered, hanging on to her weak argument with both hands.

"Even more has happened since Vic showed up. As *you* requested." Rather than try and convince

Aubrey of her part in this drama, Chelsea raised her hand to signal the waiter. "How about dessert? I want dessert."

Aubrey nodded automatically, but she didn't care if she ate dessert or not. What she cared about was her heart, her future. Her *life*.

She'd decided when she'd been in college to honor her dreams and build a life she deserved, no matter what.

Which left one nagging question: What kind of life did she want now?

Nineteen

On her way to her classroom, Aubrey was stopped no fewer than seven times by friends and coworkers.

She received hugs, well-wishes and handshakes. Everyone was welcoming and happy to see her. It felt good to be back.

"Aubrey!" Elise approached from the long, empty hallway, ever the picture of sophistication in a navy blue pencil skirt, white silk shirt and red high heels.

"You look gorgeous."

Elise gave her a quick hug. "I'd talk. Your legs are incredible."

Aubrey wore a green-and-white-striped skirt that flared at the knee, paired with a fitted white T-shirt. Her sandals were wedges with cork heels. "I was going for professional."

"You overshot the mark, my friend."

"I hope I remember how to do this." Aubrey made a face as she unlocked her classroom door.

"You were *born* to do this. One doesn't forget something that's been baked into them since birth." Elise followed her into the classroom. She chewed her lip and studied her shoes. Normally outspoken, it was odd behavior for her. "I'm sorry for not telling you the truth about Vic."

"You don't have to apologize."

"I do. As your friend, I should have taken your side. I will hate that man until the end of time out of loyalty to you." Elise cocked her head, a somewhat hopeful expression on her face. "Unless…you've forgiven him?"

"Not exactly."

She shrugged. "My vow stands."

"I appreciate your loyalty, but I'm not sure if it's that easy."

"Was that Aubrey I saw sneak in here?" Primrose walked into the classroom next and swept Aubrey into a warm hug. "We heard about Vic. That rat."

"How?" Aubrey hadn't talked to anyone about what'd happened between them except for Chelsea.

"He came here!" Primrose exclaimed. "He pulled each of us aside and apologized."

"And then he said he was in love with you." Brooke strolled in next, her lips pursed. "These two want me to hate him, but out of principle, I can't hate a man that beautiful. Even though I love you so very much."

"Thanks, Brooke." Aubrey's smile felt forced as she pictured Vic apologizing to her friends and declaring his love for her. "I don't hate him, so that seems fair."

"Really?" Primrose wrinkled her nose.

"Really." Aubrey lowered into her chair, weighed down by everything. "His sister Chelsea told me he is lost without me. She claims his behavior was because he's still in love with me."

"He should have told you he loved you," Elise stated.

"Oh, he did. He told me and gave me my engagement ring back."

Brooke gasped.

"As much as I'd love to share more, I have to refamiliarize myself with how to do my job before I have thirty sixteen-year-olds in my class."

"Good call." Primrose hustled for the door, grabbing Brooke on the way. "They are brutally honest, so mind yourself."

"Do you want some Mace?" Elise whispered. "Bear spray?"

"I'm good," Aubrey answered with a laugh. "I appreciate you all thinking of me. By the way, I don't blame any of you for playing along. I would have done the same for you, unless I believed you were in some sort of danger." Once Primrose and Brooke were gone, Aubrey met Elise's eyes. "You know Vic. If you believed he was taking advantage of me, you'd have told me."

Elise gave a reluctant nod. "I suppose you're right."

Halfway through her day, Aubrey readied herself for the next class to pour through her doors. She knew she wasn't supposed to have favorites, but this group of students had quickly risen to the top within the first three weeks of the new school year.

As the students filed in, a few left behind cards or small mementos to welcome their teacher back. Her heart lifted. She was infinitely grateful to be here and focusing her attention on something other than her eroding personal life.

"Thank you for the gifts. It's good to be back." Cheers erupted, and she held her hands out to quiet her class. "I haven't done this with every class, but you're special. I know you have questions. So ask them."

"Anything?" Brennon McCreedy asked, his thick eyebrows lifting impishly.

"Anything you would ask your mom," she retorted to much of the class's approval.

"I have a question," Jamaica Barnard, one of her star students, said.

"I'm all ears."

"Did you miss us?" She grinned.

"More than any of my other students," Aubrey mock-whispered. "Come on. I know you are curious about my amnesia."

"Is it true? Is that really why you were gone?" asked Anderson Phillips. "Sounds like bullshit."

"I agree," Aubrey said. "Amnesia happens more often than you think, but it's not common. And it wasn't something I fully understood before going through it. In my case, there were gaps in my memory, while I remembered other parts of my life vividly."

"Did your memory return all at once?" Jamaica asked.

"It was a bit of a trickle until a friend intervened.

He shared the parts that had been missing. With my doctor's permission, of course."

"He?" Madison Black waggled her eyebrows, and Aubrey's hormone-riddled class made *oooh* sounds, hinting that they thought this "he" might be romantically linked to Aubrey. "Ms. Collins, we were not aware you had a boyfriend."

"He's an old boyfriend," Aubrey admitted in spite of herself.

"Old as in geriatric?"

"No, Jacob. Old as in from my past."

"You know, like you and Ava," Madison put in.

"Burn!" Anderson pointed at Jacob, who turned a bright shade of pink.

"Did it work out?" The blunt question came from quiet, polite Mia Stoker.

"No. We see life differently. Then and now."

"Isn't that what you always tell us makes our writing strong?" Mia pressed. "Remember to—"

"'See the scene from the other person's eyes,'" the rest of the class quoted in unison.

Aubrey was both peeved and proud. "You're using my words against me."

"Have you seen things through his eyes?" Jamaica asked. "Or is he a lowly dog, like Caleb?"

"Hey!" Caleb, arguably the sweetest guy in their grade, protested. Aubrey noticed Jamaica sending him a flirty smile. Ah, teenagers.

"A story for another day, perhaps. We're running out of time, and I know you're anxious to discuss your reading assignment, yes?"

"We don't get a pass because you were gone?" Jacob asked.

"Sorry. Your substitute teacher told me that she kept you on course while I was away."

A few groans rippled through the classroom.

"But," she interjected, "I might grant you an extension if you participate in the lesson today. Raise your hand, attempt to answer, read aloud. You know, that sort of thing."

The groans this time around sounded more lighthearted than before.

"Now, open your texts to page..."

After Jayden helped Vic untangle a cow that'd wrapped its leg in barbed wire, Vic invited him over for sandwiches. They'd been hard at work all morning, and he was half-starved.

In the Grandin family kitchen, Vic thanked the kitchen staff for setting out the sandwich ingredients on the counter before dismissing them. Privacy was a hard thing to come by in this house, and something he had been craving since Aubrey had kicked him out of her apartment.

"Slumming it today, I see," Jayden joked as he grabbed a plate for himself.

"It's good to get your hands dirty every once in a while."

After a minute of them silently putting together their sandwiches, Jayden asked, "So, did you buy her something to hammer home your apology? New car? Another piece of jewelry?"

Vic didn't pretend not to know whom his friend

was referring to. He took a breath and confessed, "I bought her a house."

Jayden stared at Vic in frozen disbelief. "A house."

"Well, the same house."

"The house you bought when you were dating her? Tell me you sold that."

Vic shook his head. He probably should have sold it.

Jayden whistled long and low before taking a seat at the counter to eat his lunch. "You need therapy."

"It didn't seem right to live there without her. I couldn't bring myself to sell it, either."

"Because?"

Vic shrugged, but he knew why. "Selling it would be admitting I knew she'd never take me back."

"Damn. I cannot believe you've been this gone for this girl for this long and never told me."

"I was trying to get over her."

"Well, it didn't work," Jayden added unhelpfully before he bit into his sandwich. After he chewed and swallowed, he regarded Vic with a modicum of sincerity. "What now? Is she done with you?"

Vic winced. "I don't want to accept it, but she might be. She has the engagement ring. She hasn't given it back yet, but I'm afraid to hope." He dropped his sandwich on his plate without tasting it. "I love her, and I want to spend the rest of my life with her. I tried to prove to her that I've changed, but I fucked everything up."

"Don't be so hard on yourself, baby brother. Hey, Jayden," Chelsea greeted as she strode into the kitchen. She pulled off her work gloves and set them on the counter, surveying the spread in front of her. "Are we fending for ourselves today?"

"Apparently," Jayden grumbled.

She began building her own sandwich. "I spoke to Aubrey the other day. It didn't seem to me like she hated you."

Vic, his sandwich halfway to his mouth, dropped it on his plate again. "Tell me you're kidding."

"Not kidding. We had lunch at that cute café downtown with the—"

"Chels, this isn't any of your business."

"Like Nolan and me weren't any of yours?"

Jayden chuckled. Vic sent him a death glare.

"I care about you, okay?" His sister moved to where Vic was standing, elbowing Jayden as she passed by. "We all care about you."

"Yeah, I care, too," Jayden said around another bite.

"Are you going to the fall festival at the Texas Cattleman's Club?"

"Of course," Jayden answered at the same time Vic said, "No way."

"You have to go," Chelsea informed Vic.

"Yes, you do." Jayden polished off his sandwich and took a swig from his soda can. "You cannot leave me to my own devices. God knows what I'll do."

"You'll survive. You can bob for apples or carve pumpkins or whatever they plan on doing this year."

"What if you-know-who is there?" Chelsea asked.

"All the more reason not to go." Vic finally took a bite of his sandwich, but it sat like wet cement on his tongue, flavorless and heavy.

He *wanted* to see Aubrey. If only to figure out if she still hated him as much as she had the other day. He was too afraid to hope she didn't. If she had decided she felt nothing for him, he'd have a funeral to plan—his own. This time around, a broken heart would kill him. He was sure of it.

He'd held on to the house to keep hope alive, and he needed to know if Aubrey had held on to the engagement ring for the same reason. As long as she had it in her possession, that meant she was still possibly, *maybe* considering marrying him. If not...well, she wasn't.

He didn't know what else he could do to convince her he loved her and wanted her in his life until his dying day. Time apart hadn't helped them the first time around.

"Just go and see what happens. If she shows, she might be glad to see you." Chelsea said.

"That's very naive of you, sis. I'm surprised."

"Love can change a person. It changed you. I barely recognize you anymore."

"Hear, hear." Jayden held up his soda can and toasted Chelsea's glass of water. "He used to be a beast. Now he's a puppy."

"I'm eating in my room," Vic grumbled, tired of everyone's input on what had happened between him and Aubrey.

Once he'd closed himself in his suite, he pulled out his cell phone to check his texts. Nothing. The last five he'd sent to Aubrey had gone unanswered.

He sent one more anyway.

Twenty

Another text appeared on Aubrey's phone screen, beneath the previous five she hadn't answered. Not that Vic had asked a question. He hadn't said, "I miss you" or "I love you" or trotted out multiple apologies. Each of his five texts was as random as they came, the tone casual, like when he and Aubrey were dating, talking to and seeing each other every day.

The latest entry into the diary of Vic's day read, These tomatoes are damn good. I know you don't typically eat them, but they're stripey and sort of sweet. Jayden is being a prick. Why are we best friends, again? Chelsea, meanwhile, is being sweet. It's weird.

Aubrey read it twice, tempted to respond. She could tell him how, stripey or not, she wasn't interested in *any* tomato. Or she could explain that he was best friends with Jayden because no other male understood Vic better. On the Chelsea front, she longed to encourage him to embrace his oldest sister's doting.

Aubrey understood why Chelsea had crashed the lunch she'd intended to have by herself. Chelsea loved her family, loved the ranch and cared about Aubrey a great deal. As an only child, Aubrey saw the value of having an interfering sibling.

But responding would give Vic false hope, and she didn't want to hurt him further. She didn't want him to believe all was forgiven because he'd sent several texts as if nothing was wrong.

Everything was wrong.

She parked in her parents' driveway and stepped onto the porch. Normally she'd let herself in, but she hesitated at the front door. After she'd drawn a hard line with them, she wasn't sure how welcome she'd be here.

Mary Collins answered the door, her red hair pulled off her face and tied into a short ponytail. Her freckles were out in droves. She appeared tired, if a little fragile. Aubrey's heart hurt.

"Hi, Mom."

"Aubrey. It's good to see you." Mary held up the dish towel in her hand. "I was cleaning the kitchen and swearing because I couldn't reach the cabinet above the refrigerator. How are you?"

"I'm…" Aubrey wanted to say "fine" or "okay" but decided to tell the truth instead. A truth that caused her chin to wobble and her eyes to heat. "I'm overflowing with regret."

"Oh, honey, come in here." Mary tugged her daughter into the house and sat her down at the kitchen table. "Coffee will fix it."

Aubrey let out a watery laugh. She wasn't sure coffee would fix it, but she was willing to try.

Five minutes later, two mugs of coffee on the table in front of them, Aubrey apologized to her mother. "I was harsh and unreasonable."

"You've been through a lot."

"I love you and Dad so much. I never should have said the awful things I said before I left. And not speaking to you…what if something terrible had happened to you or him, and the last thing I said to you was—" She hiccupped and covered her mouth, not willing to finish that sentence.

"Nothing has happened. Your father's at the home improvement store. He's perfectly fine. I know, because he's called me twice and asked me to measure the shelves in the garage. He's on a mission to completely reorganize." Her mother rolled her eyes. "We figured you didn't mean it, Aub. Your father knows you. He was the one who told Vic to give you time. You needed to be alone, and we respected that."

"Vic was here?"

"The day he dropped you off and you went to your room to pack. He came to the door."

Of course he did.

"He's come to see me since then, too."

"Did he?"

"He says he loves me. He wants a second chance. I guess if I say yes, it would be a *third* chance. I'm not willing to do that. Or I wasn't, anyway. Until my students reminded me how I taught them the most successful storytellers see life from the other characters' points of view as well as their own. Then I started thinking about how Vic must have felt for the last ten years. And about how he felt when he was asked to pretend to date me because being with him was one of the last things I remembered." Hands around her coffee mug, she spoke to her mother more earnestly than she'd intended. "We slept together the night before the chili cook-off."

Mary's cheeks went pink, but she didn't try and stop Aubrey from sharing.

"It was supposed to be one night. I saw him at the bar at the Silver Saddle, and he was so familiar. Like the boy I dated. Except he was a man, and there were only good parts left. He seemed so grown-up. So different from before. And I had an escape hatch—one night to be with the Vic I used to love, and then I could return to my regularly scheduled life." She shook her head at her own naivete. As if one night with Vic wouldn't be burned into her memory forever—hell, that single memory had survived while countless others had temporarily perished.

"That night was so…intense," she continued. "The emotions I thought were long gone returned and made themselves at home. Nothing but positive feelings for him remained after I lost my memory. It's like I forgot everything bad that happened in the four years we dated."

"There wasn't much bad, Aub. You two had a lot of wonderful years together. At the end, you had a disagreement."

“A disagreement? We had totally different life plans.” Aubrey nested her fingers into her hair.

“Honey.” Mary touched Aubrey’s arm. “You did the right thing then, and I’ll never not back you on that. You wanted to focus on school and attain your degrees. You wanted to live your life untethered. Who could blame you? So, now that you’ve been untethered for ten years, what do you want? Do you want to reclaim the life you had before with Vic, or do you want to move forward and chalk up the days you spent with him as a learning experience? It sounds like both options are on the table. All you have to do is choose one.”

Aubrey gave her mother a beseeching look. “Choose one. As if it’s that simple?”

Her mother patted Aubrey’s arm. “It’s not simple. But your father and I will back you no matter which one you choose.”

“You look like dog shit.” Vic’s youngest sister, Morgan, entered his office and plopped onto the sofa. She crossed her legs, tugging at the skirt of a stylish dress, no doubt from her shop.

“Won’t you come in.” He shut his laptop and rubbed his eyes. It was noon, and he’d been at it for six hours already.

“I brought you something to cheer you up,” Morgan said, ignoring his sarcasm. She hopped off the sofa and ran into the hallway, returning with her fingers looped around the handle of a paper bag half the size of his desk.

“I already ate.”

"Open it, smart-ass."

He unearthed the contents: a shirt, suit jacket, dark-wash jeans and a new belt. Holding up the silver buckle with the Grandin family ranch's logo on it, he sent Morgan a questioning look. "It's October. Too early for Christmas."

"It's not a Christmas gift. It's for you to wear to the fall festival at the TCC."

He piled the clothing back into the bag. "I'm not going."

"You have to go. I bought you all this stuff!"

"First off, you have a million connections in the clothing industry who would gift you anything you asked for."

She blushed, hinting that while she might have spent time selecting the pieces, she certainly hadn't spent money.

"Second, I don't need it, because I'm not going. Thirdly, Chelsea and Jayden have already been bothering me about going, and I told them no, too."

"It's tomorrow. You *have* to go. Actually, we all have to go. Daddy's orders."

"What's he going to do, fire me?"

"Working all hours of the day and night isn't going to speed up the process of finding out if there's oil under our property. And it's also not going to heal your heart."

"If you don't mind—" he reopened his laptop "—I have some invoices to finalize."

Morgan slapped his laptop shut and regarded him with redheaded ire. "I remember what you were like back when you and Aubrey broke up."

"I was a jackass. That's what I was like."

"That's what everyone thought. But I saw the truth. You were heartbroken. You were sad and you cried and told no one. Then you were withdrawn. Then you were angry and short-tempered. When you and Jayden went out to pick up women, you were gross. You pretended like being a playboy was your favorite pastime, but that's not you, Vic."

He'd had no idea she'd been paying such close attention, or he might've behaved better. The idea that his youngest sister, who had always looked up to him, had found him "gross" and seen through his actions made him feel slightly sick.

"Whenever you were out all night, you never came home the next morning looking happy. I saw you at a TCC event with another girl more times than I can count, and your smile was fake. Admit it. You are not complete without Aubrey Collins."

"I tried, okay?" he snapped, because the truth fucking hurt.

"*Not* okay. What's your plan? To sit around and wait for another ten years?"

"She's not interested in what I have to say, Morgan!" His voice lifted out of frustration. Every one of his previous attempts to reach Aubrey had been futile. She was icing him. It was over.

"So you're going to be like this again." His sister gestured to his slumped posture. "You're going to be sad and withdrawn. Or angry and short-tempered. You're going to date miscellaneous women and be unhappy."

"I'm not dating anyone."

“So you’re going to be single and unhappy.”

“You’re single, and you’re not unhappy.”

“I’m not in love with my ex.” She cocked her head and hoisted an eyebrow. “Go to the festival. You need a night away, to feel something other than regret. Plus, you’re wrong. I special-ordered the belt buckle and paid for it with my own money. It’s not returnable.”

She turned on her boot heel and clomped out of his office.

Vic sighed as he moved the paper bag from desktop to floor. What difference a fall festival was going to make, he had no idea. He’d figured out at least one benefit to going, however—it’d get his siblings and his friend off his back.

“Knock, knock.” Layla entered his office next.

“I’m going to the fall festival,” he announced before she started in on him. “I’m going to bob for apples and pin the tail on the scarecrow or whatever shit they do there. I’ll take first prize for whatever contest they hold. Are you happy?”

Layla’s eyebrows climbed her forehead. “The contest they’re having is for the best needlepoint. I’ve seen your clumsy fingers, brother. I doubt you could create anything that would final.”

A reluctant smile crept across his lips. He scratched his cheek. “Sorry. It’s been a morning.”

“I don’t care if you go to the fall festival or not.” Layla knelt to dig through the bag on the floor. She held up the suit jacket. “This is nice.”

“Morgan.”

“I saw her. She’s on a mission.”

"Everyone is. It's Operation Help Vic Because He's a Pathetic Bastard."

"You're not a pathetic bastard." She patted his head. "You're lovesick and giving up. Which, I guess, is another way to say you're a pathetic bastard. So, in a way, you're right."

"I didn't give up."

"No?"

"I know you think I should skywrite Aubrey's name over her apartment complex, or buy her a horse and tie it to her car, but she deserves to have the space I didn't give her after her accident. She's the woman she grew into without me. She's incredible. And she broke up with me to become that woman. I can't demand she take me back. I tried demanding when we split up the first time around. All I managed to do was create a rift between us that was irreparable."

"I doubt that." Layla cocked her blond head. "You two were behaving like you loved each other from what I could see. She's not the same Aubrey who dumped you, true. She's an adult who knows her heart and mind. She is intelligent and thoughtful. Even if she was missing a memory or two while you were sleeping together and making out in the stable—"

He sent her a warning look that didn't slow her down in the least.

"—she knew in her heart that you were meant for her, and she was meant for you."

"I want to believe that, Lay, I do. But—"

"Then believe it. Lose this hangdog thing you have going on." She tossed the suit jacket on his lap. "Walk into the fall festival with your head held high. You're the sole male Grandin of your generation, Vic. You're a catch. Aubrey would be a lucky woman to have a man like you loving her for the rest of her life."

He narrowed his eyes at his sister. "There something else you want? It would explain the abject flattery."

"You to be happy, baby bro. That's enough." She offered a sincere smile, blew him a kiss and stepped out of his office.

Twenty-One

The Texas Cattleman's Club used to be an old-school men's club, through and through. Built around 1910, the large, rambling, single-story building had been ground zero for too many parties to count. From the dark wood floors to the leather-upholstered furniture and the high, regal ceilings, the TCC made for a lush backdrop for any festivity.

After the club began admitting female members over a decade ago, things started to change for the better. Helping lure in a younger demographic were parents demanding their children's attendance, as well as a recent renovation. Newly added windows brought much-needed light to the space, and there were splashes of color where there'd been earth tones before.

Tonight the decor was autumn leaves, pumpkins

and tall cornstalks adorned with fancy ribbons. Vic didn't see apple bobbing or pumpkin carving, but he'd bet they were doing that in the on-site day care.

His sister Morgan had kept a close eye on him tonight. She had stopped by the house to fuss over his wardrobe and then demanded he drive her to the event. He suspected that was so she could further ensure he showed up, but he hadn't protested.

Being here wasn't as bad as he'd thought. He'd spent a long, frustrating week at his desk poring over spreadsheets or on the phone with countless suppliers. While the Grandin family home was as large as five decent-size homes, the walls had begun to feel as if they were closing in on him.

The bartender handed over his glass of whiskey. Vic turned and knocked his glass against Jayden's. "Go hunt," he teased his best friend before taking a sip. "No sense in wasting your evening hanging around with me."

"True story. You're a downer." Jayden caught the eye of a woman across the room, her smile as dazzling as her short, sparkling dress. "Looks like I'm up."

"Have fun." One of them should.

Vic wandered through the well-dressed crowd, pretending not to look for the only woman who could turn his head nowadays. Then, on his second pass, he spotted her.

Aubrey was wearing a floor-length, autumnal red-orange dress, gold bangle bracelets stacked on one wrist. From her auburn hair to her strappy gold shoes, she was fall personified, like the burnished leaves on an oak tree at the height of the season. Her lips were painted reddish-brown, her smile, while not beaming, polite for anyone who approached. From the looks of it, she hadn't made it far past the entrance—and wouldn't anytime soon, given the crowd surrounding her.

No doubt the men and women forming a semicircle around her were curious about Aubrey's accident and her subsequent miraculous recovery. She'd arrived alone, from the looks of it. Being new to the club, with her honorary membership, she had yet to learn how to politely disentangle herself from the crowd.

He paced back to the bar and ordered a glass of chardonnay and then, wineglass in hand, he inserted himself directly between the regular club members and Aubrey. Her expressive green eyes widened in surprise when he offered her the drink.

"If you'll excuse us." He didn't offer further explanation, but he did offer Aubrey his arm. After a reluctant beat, she laid her hand on his forearm. In what felt like the most natural move ever, he led her to the other side of the room, his heart pounding fiercely with each step he took.

He stopped in a quiet corner near a sizable modern painting. "I thought you might need to catch your breath, or at least have a drink before answering a zillion medical and personal questions from every busybody in the county."

"Thanks. I was trapped." Her laugh caused his chest to tighten. He hadn't been sure she'd appreciate his intervening, but it seemed she had.

She sipped her wine as music drifted through the room. It reminded him of the night at the botanical gardens, when he'd held her and she'd shared what she remembered from prom night. That felt like an eternity ago already.

"Any word about the issues with the ranch?" she asked.

He shook his head. "Alexa updated us on where the PI is with the investigation. There's been a new development, but no one knows anything for sure. Except that Heath believes his mother was bribed with oil rights. The PI is searching for paperwork."

"That must be hard for you. Knowing your future could change on a dime, and work like nothing has changed."

Her sincere gaze was the least surprising thing about her. She'd always thought of him, of his well-being, first. How he'd ever accused her of being selfish was beyond him.

"It's not as hard as losing you a second time," he told her. There was no going back now. Ever since his sisters and Jayden had given him hell about being a miserable sack, Vic had done a lot of thinking. He'd decided that as long as he was drawing air, he'd remind Aubrey how much she meant to him. He wouldn't stop unless she told him she didn't love him anymore. Until then, she was going to have to endure him.

She pressed her lips together, and he couldn't tell if her expression was embarrassment or sadness or something else entirely.

He smiled at the floor. "I'm thinking of moving out of the ranch. Know any good neighborhoods?"

"Just one," she said. "It's a beautiful neighborhood. Ideal, really."

He shut his eyes against the flood of memories. It was his turn to be pummeled by everything he'd rather not recall. In his case, every *I love you* she had offered during their second chance. Every soft moan and pleasured sigh that had escaped her mouth when they'd made love. Every hand-holding moment or beaming smile she'd given him before he'd forced himself to tell her the truth.

When he lifted his head, she was watching him. *Not* like she hated him. Her expression was soft and open, the darkness behind her eyes missing. She'd come to a conclusion. He knew it in his gut.

His rotten, sinking gut.

She set her wineglass on the small table next to them. From the small clutch she carried, she pulled out a familiar velvet box. "I, um, I brought the engagement ring."

Fuck, I knew it.

His heart stopped, sputtered and restarted its clumsy rhythm. He had instinctively known coming here tonight would result in a conclusion. He could deal with Aubrey's rejection one of two ways—he could beg her to change her mind, or he could accept that she'd made the decision that was best for her. He'd given her time. He'd given her his best reasons to say yes to him.

"I respect your decision, Aub."

"You do?" Her eyebrows lifted into her wavy hair. Auburn surrounding a face he would have liked to look into for the rest of his days.

"I do. That might surprise you, given how I tried to talk you into doing things my way when we were kids, but believe it or not, I've changed. I respect you. I love you. Still. But I won't stand in your way when your mind's made up. Just promise me—" he offered a wan smile "—if I hit my head and lose my memory, you'll tell me the truth at the start about us being a couple."

"Of course I will." Her tone was mild as she offered the box. A box that might as well weigh a metric ton for the strength it took out of his arm when he accepted it. "I love you, too, Vic."

"I understand," he said automatically. "I never should have expected you to…" He blinked at the box in his hand and then at the woman in front of him. "What did you say?"

This smile was his favorite Aubrey smile. The beaming one. "Of course I'll tell everyone we're a couple if you forget. Because we will be."

He was hardly able to believe his ears.

She adjusted the collar of his jacket, smoothing the lapels with both hands. His field of vision was filled with her: red, red and more red. From her dress to her hair to the lips he wanted to kiss more than anything.

"I thought about everything you said," she told him. "And everything Chelsea said. And everything my mom said." She rolled her eyes playfully. "We aren't the same people who split up ten years ago. I'm not the headstrong woman who wanted to do everything by myself. You're not the man with world domination in mind. I've learned that family is everything and that my life is so, so much better with you in it. Whenever I picture my future, I see two things—me, teaching until I'm old and gray and as sassy as ever."

He had to grin. She had enough sass to last her two lifetimes.

"And coming home to you and our house, with the curved hallway and the rich wood floors, after a day of teaching."

He closed his eyes, unwilling to wake up from the hallucination he was surely having. That's when he felt it. Her lips on his. Soft and plush, and pressing into him with an insistence he'd been praying for every night since he'd told her what she'd so inconveniently forgotten.

He lost her lips too soon.

"I brought you this." She took the box from his hand and held it between them. "To ask if you wanted to put it on my finger."

He narrowed one eye. "You didn't fall and hit your head again, did you?"

"No. I remember everything, Vic. You coming to my apartment to say some of the sweetest words I've ever heard. You taking me to our dream home, which you held on to for ten years in the hopes I'd come back. The loft. The stable. The shower. Your bed…"

"Okay, okay." He gripped her waist and pulled her close to him, inhaling her light, familiar scent. His Aubrey. For real, this time. For good. "If you don't want me to limp out of here, you're going to have to stop talking dirty."

He opened the velvet box of the ring that used to sit at home on Aubrey's hand. A ring that, like the dream house he'd bought her, had sat untouched for ten years. A ring that, until this very moment, he'd believed she was returning with an apology instead of an *I love you*.

"I don't have anything fancy to say." He dropped to

one knee and looked up at the only woman he'd ever loved. Around them, the room hushed, conversations trailing off into muted whispers. He ignored them and focused on Aubrey. "Will you be my wife, and move into our dream home, and teach until you're old and gray, and let me love you for the rest of my life?"

Tears welled in her eyes as she nodded. He slid the diamond onto her ring finger and then stood. Applause rippled through the room. With the thumb of the hand cradling her cheek, he swiped away a lone tear. "I love you, Aubrey."

"I love you, Vic."

He kissed her as cheers joined the applause around them. But he wasn't thinking about the crowd or the questions that would follow. He wasn't even thinking about what would happen after they left the party and he could finally be alone with his future bride.

He touched the ring on her left hand, thinking of one word: *home*.

He'd finally found where he belonged. He loved his family ranch, but his home wasn't on the Grandin estate. Not any longer. His home was in the arms of the woman who'd given him more chances than he'd deserved. The woman who'd returned to him against all odds.

He'd happily spend the rest of his life reminding her of the reasons he loved her so that she never forgot a single one again.

* * * * *

Don't miss the next installment of
Texas Cattleman's Club: Ranchers and Rivals

Cinderella Masquerade
by LaQuette

Available November 2022

COMING NEXT MONTH FROM

HARLEQUIN

DESIRE

#2905 THE OUTLAW'S CLAIM

Westmoreland Legacy: The Outlaws • by Brenda Jackson

Rancher Maverick Outlaw and Sapphire Bordella are friends with occasional benefits. But when Phire must marry at her father's urging, their relationship ends...until they learn she's carrying Maverick's baby. Now he'll stop at nothing to stake his claim...

#2906 CINDERELLA MASQUERADE

Texas Cattleman's Club: Ranchers and Rivals • by LaQuette

Ready to break out of her shell, Dr. Zanai James agrees to go all out for the town's masquerade ball and meets handsome rancher Jayden Lattimore. Their attraction is instantaneous, but can their connection survive meddling families bent on keeping them apart?

#2907 MARRIED BY MIDNIGHT

Dynasties: Tech Tycoons • by Shannon McKenna

Ronnie Moss is in trouble. The brilliant television host needs a last-minute husband to fulfill her family's marriage mandate before she turns thirty—at midnight. Then comes sexy stranger Wes Brody, who volunteers himself. But is this convenient arrangement too good to be true?

#2908 SNOWED IN SECRETS

Angel's Share • by Jules Bennett

After distillery owner Sara Hawthorne and Ian Ford spend one hot night together, they don't expect to see each other again...until he shows up for their scheduled interview about her family business. Now snowed in, can they keep it professional?

#2909 WHAT HAPPENS AFTER HOURS

404 Sound • by Kianna Alexander

Recording studio exec Miles Woodson needs a showstopping act for his charity talent show, and R & B superstar Cambria Harding fits the bill. But when long days working together become steamy nights, can these opposites make both their passion project and relationship work?

#2910 BAD BOY WITH BENEFITS

The Kane Heirs • by Cynthia St. Aubin

Sent to audit his distillery, Marlowe Kane should keep her distance from bad boy owner Law Renaud. But when a storm prevents her from getting home, they can't resist, and their relationship awakens a passion in both that could cost them everything...

YOU CAN FIND MORE INFORMATION ON UPCOMING HARLEQUIN TITLES, FREE EXCERPTS AND MORE AT HARLEQUIN.COM.

HDCNM0922

SPECIAL EXCERPT FROM

HARLEQUIN

DESIRE

Returning to her hometown, brokenhearted journalist Adaline Harlow is supposed to write an exposé on Colter Ward, Texas's Sexiest Bachelor, and that assignment does not include falling for him! As the attraction grows, will they break their no-love-allowed rule for a second chance at happiness?

Read on for a sneak peek at Most Eligible Cowboy *by* USA TODAY *bestselling author Stacey Kennedy.*

"You want your story. I want these women off my back… Stay in town and agree to being my girlfriend until this story dies down and I'll give you the exclusive you want."

"Her eyes widened. "You're serious?"

"Deadly serious," he confirmed. "I want my life back. You need a promotion. This is a win-win for both of us."

She gave a cute wiggle on her stool. "I think you're giving me far too much credit. Why would women care if I'm your girlfriend?"

"I don't think you're giving yourself enough credit." He stared at her parted lips, shining eyes, her slowly building smile, and closed the distance between them, waiting for her to back away. When she didn't and even leaned in closer, he said, "Trust me, they'd care." He captured her mouth, cupping her warm face, telling himself the whole damn time this was a terrible idea.

Don't miss what happens next in...
Most Eligible Cowboy
by USA TODAY *bestselling author Stacey Kennedy.*

Available November 2022 wherever
Harlequin Desire books and ebooks are sold.

Harlequin.com

HDEXP0922

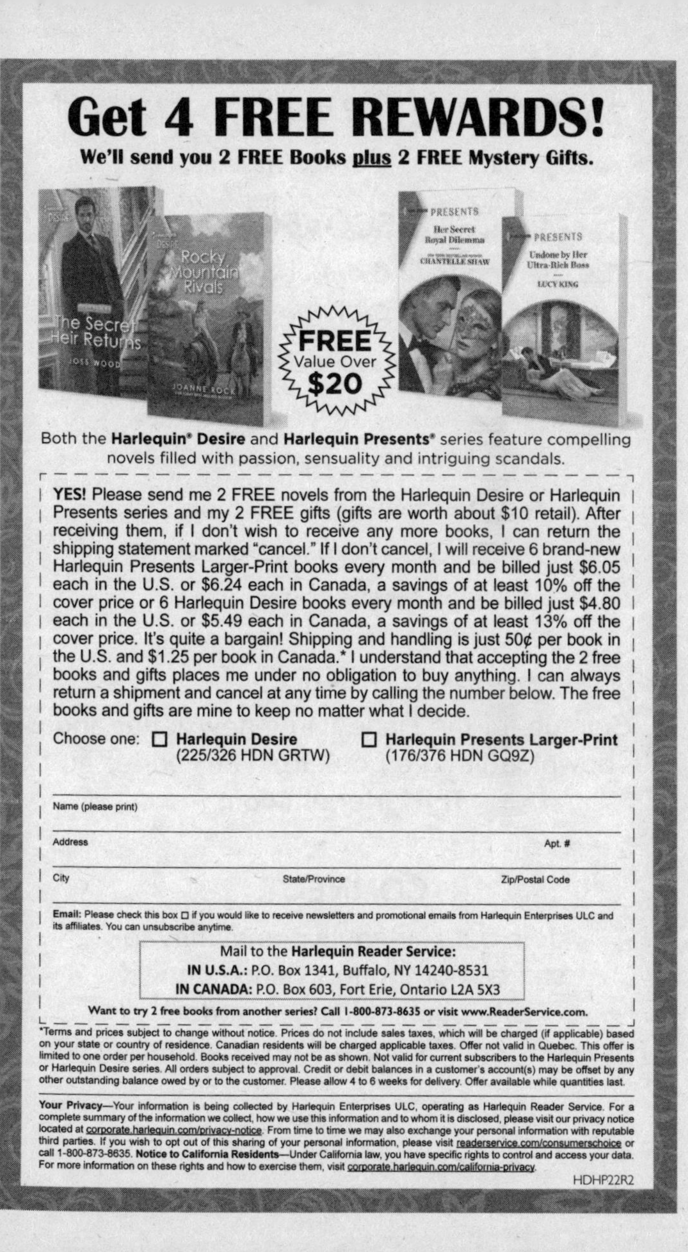
Get 4 FREE REWARDS!
We'll send you 2 FREE Books plus 2 FREE Mystery Gifts.
DESIRE
The Secret Heir Returns
JOSS WOOD
DESIRE
Rocky Mountain Rivals
JOANNE ROCK
FREE
Value Over
$20
PRESENTS
Her Secret Royal Dilemma
CHANTELLE SHAW
PRESENTS
Undone by Her Ultra-Rich Boss
LUCY KING
Both the Harlequin® Desire and Harlequin Presents® series feature compelling novels filled with passion, sensuality and intriguing scandals.
YES! Please send me 2 FREE novels from the Harlequin Desire or Harlequin Presents series and my 2 FREE gifts (gifts are worth about $10 retail). After receiving them, if I don't wish to receive any more books, I can return the shipping statement marked "cancel." If I don't cancel, I will receive 6 brand-new Harlequin Presents Larger-Print books every month and be billed just $6.05 each in the U.S. or $6.24 each in Canada, a savings of at least 10% off the cover price or 6 Harlequin Desire books every month and be billed just $4.80 each in the U.S. or $5.49 each in Canada, a savings of at least 13% off the cover price. It's quite a bargain! Shipping and handling is just 50¢ per book in the U.S. and $1.25 per book in Canada.* I understand that accepting the 2 free books and gifts places me under no obligation to buy anything. I can always return a shipment and cancel at any time by calling the number below. The free books and gifts are mine to keep no matter what I decide.
Choose one: ☐ Harlequin Desire (225/326 HDN GRTW) ☐ Harlequin Presents Larger-Print (176/376 HDN GQ9Z)
Name (please print)
Address
Apt. #
City
State/Province
Zip/Postal Code
Email: Please check this box ☐ if you would like to receive newsletters and promotional emails from Harlequin Enterprises ULC and its affiliates. You can unsubscribe anytime.
Mail to the Harlequin Reader Service:
IN U.S.A.: P.O. Box 1341, Buffalo, NY 14240-8531
IN CANADA: P.O. Box 603, Fort Erie, Ontario L2A 5X3
Want to try 2 free books from another series? Call 1-800-873-8635 or visit www.ReaderService.com.
*Terms and prices subject to change without notice. Prices do not include sales taxes, which will be charged (if applicable) based on your state or country of residence. Canadian residents will be charged applicable taxes. Offer not valid in Quebec. This offer is limited to one order per household. Books received may not be as shown. Not valid for current subscribers to the Harlequin Presents or Harlequin Desire series. All orders subject to approval. Credit or debit balances in a customer's account(s) may be offset by any other outstanding balance owed by or to the customer. Please allow 4 to 6 weeks for delivery. Offer available while quantities last.
Your Privacy—Your information is being collected by Harlequin Enterprises ULC, operating as Harlequin Reader Service. For a complete summary of the information we collect, how we use this information and to whom it is disclosed, please visit our privacy notice located at corporate.harlequin.com/privacy-notice. From time to time we may also exchange your personal information with reputable third parties. If you wish to opt out of this sharing of your personal information, please visit readerservice.com/consumerschoice or call 1-800-873-8635. Notice to California Residents—Under California law, you have specific rights to control and access your data. For more information on these rights and how to exercise them, visit corporate.harlequin.com/california-privacy.
HDHP22R2